D0935888

THE
WORLD
IS A
ROOM *and other stories*

TRANSLATED FROM
THE HEBREW BY
Elinor Grumet
Hillel Halkin
Ada Hameirit-Sarell
Jules Harlow
Yosef Schachter

The Jewish Publication Society of America
Philadelphia   5744 / 1984

THE WORLD IS A ROOM

and other stories by

YEHUDA AMICHAI

© 1984 by The Jewish Publication Society of America
Hebrew text copyright Schocken, Tel Aviv.
All rights reserved. Manufactured in the United States of America.

Library of Congress Cataloging in Publication Data
Amichai, Yehuda.
   The world is a room and other stories.
   Translation of selections from: Ba-ruaḥ ha-nora' ah
ha-zot.
   Contents: The snow—Dicky's death—Nina of
Ashkelon—[etc.]
   I. Title.
PJ5054.A65B35213   1984   892.4'36   83-24881
ISBN 0-8276-0234-0

Design: ADRIANNE ONDERDONK DUDDEN

CONTENTS

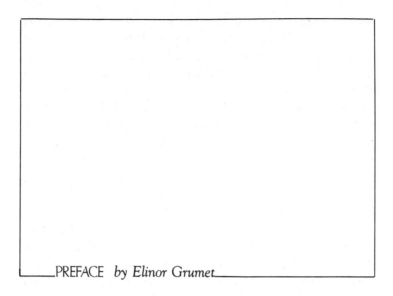

PREFACE *by Elinor Grumet*

Yehuda Amichai's stories take the liberty of poems: their
structure grows by the juxtaposition of metaphor, their
meaning clarifies in the accumulating feeling of imagery.
Amichai himself conceived of his stories as poems that
needed more space to complete themselves. Although there
is action, his stories are not plotted in the usual sense. They
are tellings, not tales. Some, entirely episodic—like "The
Snow"—have the quality of dreams. These stories take a
structural risk.

John Gardner has suggested that good fiction contains
something elusive, something of our human mysteriousness.
Reading Amichai, one feels the mystery of a simplicity
bearing great contradiction. And among the tensions, this
is one of the most compelling: the writer's work of imagi-

nation heals while it intensifies the pain of adulthood. A recurrent obsession of Amichai's work is the longing for human connectedness and the adult truth of its impossibility. (That truth is the real initiation of "The Bar Mitzvah Party.") A nameless, wounded character walks through the stories. He is displaced, trying to write, to love; or to cope with the events of war or death; or to recover a home. "You have to change him like a picture on the wall," the women in "The Orgy" say of the aimless man they know. And the narrator of "Terrible Spring," carrying around a bag of possible identities, is only saved by friends who are finally home to let him in. Most of the stories uncover the ways in which love fails to address the great need for human connection.

But imagination sets to work to heal the pain of dissociation. Amichai undertakes to negotiate what is difficult to bear with fresh imagery. There is a need to lighten grief and frailty by associating them with things that have already been domesticated. Consider this image from "Love in Reverse":

He saw his life as an Haftorah that is read on the Sabbath in the synagogue, which he had attended as a child. The Haftorah must contain some allusion to what is written in the portion for that day. Sometimes a slight allusion is sufficient, merely the name of a person or a place. His life was like that, with only slight, superficial hints of his true life.

The wit of analogy takes the sting out of the proposition. And it is this wit that drives Amichai's fiction, his way of bargaining with difficulty.

On the other hand, Amichai uses a familiar image to intensify a difficult feeling to the point of dread. The image of innocent play, for example, is used to that effect in "The World is a Room":

Once he surprised her, and without her sensing him approach from behind, he put the palms of his hands over her eyes. "Guess who." And she, even though she knew who it was, didn't give the right answer. Similarly, fate would sometimes come to them and say "Guess who," and they would guess and guess: They guessed names of enemies and lovers and others, but they never guessed whose hand it really was. So the palms of the hands of fate remained on their eyes and they were blind.

This disturbing wit, and Amichai's rapid-fire gift for analogy itself, work to heighten the reader's sense of distress, of lost connection. In the examples above, a child's game and tradition are available for metaphor precisely because they stand so readily dissociated from their contexts. Imagination may heal and refresh but, throwing before us a miscellany of pictures, it shows itself to be a symptom of the disengagement the writer feels most deeply, and which is his recurrent subject.

Then again, by their sheer number, Amichai's metaphors make us happy. All the pictures suggest that life is miscellaneous and possible. The power of the literary conceit in Amichai's hands may be measured by his ability in these stories to build structures of diverse comparisons, arousing conflicting attitudes, that are resolved euphoniously in feeling.

Despite so fundamental a complexity, the effect of these stories is finally one of great simplicity. "And maybe that is one of the functions of real poetry: To open, to inflame, to confuse and then again to close, to order and assuage." Amichai wrote this, speculating about the work of W. H. Auden. It is a description equally useful in describing the emotional effect of his own work.

The governing simplicity in these stories has something to do with Amichai's faith in the constant act of interpreting, of meeting the world in thought. The generous spirit his work radiates is partly due to his fascination with preoccupation itself; he recognizes it, dwells on it. The narrator of "Dicky's Death" recalls a detail of his service in the War of Independence: "In the sorghum field on the other side of the white wadi we used to advance across a long exposed front, boys and girls separately. We would advance that way to the horizon. I loved to sit at the horizon's edge and meditate; we were living like the other small animals. There was no harm in it." These stories are filled with homage to daydreaming, and with respect for obsessive thinking, by which people are in large part determined.

There were times when [my father's] thoughts overburdened his small body, and he sagged under their load. And there were times when he stood firm and strong like a chain of telephone wires. Even the songbirds would then alight and perch on them. [From "The Times My Father Died"]

The stories in this volume were written in the 1950s and represent half the original collection *In This Terrible Wind*, which was published in 1961. The history of Amichai's times are here: the evening Palestine was partitioned, the Israeli War of Independence, the early years of the State. It's truer to say that historic events are here only in refraction, domesticated. "I tried to go out into my times, and to know," Amichai wrote in his long poem-cycle *Travels of a Latter-Day Benjamin of Tudela*, "but I didn't get further/than the woman's body beside me."

There is one recurring experience characteristic of modern Israeli society that is close to Amichai's way of experiencing: an endlessly episodic preparation for battle, odd in its only slight dissociation from daily life. It is an activity both pointed and random in which emotion is high, but has no steady object. "Battle for the Hill" takes the anxiety of military preparation as its subject and, arousing a fine and unusual balance of emotion, is one of the most perfectly realized stories in this collection.

Wellesley, Massachusetts
April 1984

THE
WORLD
IS A
ROOM   *and other stories*

BATTLE FOR THE HILL

This story is set in Jerusalem during the Sinai Campaign of 1956, when the city, protected by thousands of suddenly mobilized citizen-soldiers, waited five long days for a war which never came. The title is itself an ironic comment on the countless war stories with similar names which have filled Israel's periodicals during the past two decades.

My wife and I crossed the street which led to where our friends live. We passed by the leper hospital, but as usual I failed to see a single one of the white invalids among the old trees. You never see them. The gates are always open, footsteps have trodden the grass and wheels have flattened it, but one never sees a soul. Sometimes you see milk cans standing before one of the iron doors sunk deep within the wall. I have yet to see a milkman.

One day last winter I stood beside this same wall and took refuge from a sudden cloudburst. I stood under the small corrugated roof which projects from it at an angle. I have no idea why the slanting roof was built. I stood fixed beneath it like a holy icon in some Christian land. Standing there, I watched the last fugitives fleeing from the rain and listened to the noise they made as they splashed through the puddles.

Now, however, a soldier stood near the wall. I watched him gesture with his hands as if he were directing traffic. There were no cars within sight or hearing, but I spotted a young woman crossing a field covered with rocks and briars. The soldier motioned to her with his hands, and I heard him call out: "More to the right, that's it, and now to the left again. No, no! Not towards me. Away from me. That's right, that's right." The woman obeyed his directions, growing smaller until she disappeared; I doubt if she will ever see him again, or if he will see her.

Our friends live on a plot of land which is not theirs and in a house which is not theirs. The armchair in the living room has finally been repaired, and the bay window is at rest at last. It is recessed and placid, like a gulf into which ships no longer venture. For the first time in years the iron gate was open. The wash was hung out to dry; shirts and pants swayed freed of the body, like our thoughts, which are formed in our bodies but sometimes fly free in the wind. My friend's wife runs a kindergarten. The front yard contained a playground: a slide and a tiny ladder for make-believe angels. The children push and shove each other until they reach the top. The pleasure of sliding down lasts no longer than a second. A small boy, who seemed to have been forgotten from the day before, stood there holding a red balloon in his hands. An old car, stripped of its wheels and motor and painted red, rested in the sand for the children to play with. In a like manner, the ideas of my forefathers have come down to me: just the frame with a bright coat of paint. Sometimes it seems that I sit in them, or play with them, but I never go anywhere.

The army runner came looking for me. The same soldier I had seen giving directions to his wife turned out to be the runner of my company, who had been dispatched to bring me in. He is always on the run, with some message in his hand or mouth. Now I spied him coming down the walled-in road. A piece of white paper fluttered in his hands like a captured butterfly. He caught up with me as I stood in the playground beside the painted car. Gasping and panting, he halted before me short of breath, looking the way runners are supposed to look. I read what was written on the paper. Instead of going on to see our friends, I sat my wife down in the sandbox next to the forgotten boy, and proceeded to the mobilization room at the army base. I passed through many rooms: the buffet, the engineering corps room, the synagogue, the quartermaster's room, the bathroom—until finally I came to the mobilization room. There I expected to find a great bustle of people, coming and going in a hurry, but I found only two women soldiers sitting in front of the door. "Wait just a minute!" they said in unison as I approached, and then settled down again. One of them wore a blouse with a flower pattern and a khaki skirt, the other a khaki blouse and a skirt with a flower pattern—like clowns at Purim. It had all happened suddenly. One of them had been on leave and had just had time to put on her khaki blouse again when there came a knock on her front door. The other was preparing to go on leave and had already removed her army skirt when they knocked on *her* door. In the confusion she had snatched the skirt with the flower pattern that was draped over the back of a chair, and had put it on, holding it tight with both hands because she couldn't find the zipper.

"We weren't expecting this."

"We weren't ready."

"Can I go in now?"

"One moment. What's the rush? You'll get there."

"We weren't ready. It happened so suddenly."

"It always comes suddenly."

"The bottom of your slip is showing."

"I know. It's too long for the khaki skirt."

"When I'm in uniform, I don't wear my slip."

"Too bad."

"We just weren't ready."

Then I heard the sound of chairs being moved about inside the room. Distant doors opened and slammed shut, and heavy footsteps resounded through the building.

"You can enter now. Come in!" said a voice from within.

It was getting on toward evening. The last rays of sunshine slanted through the drawn blinds, staining my forehead with a golden light. I wiped the stains from my forehead like beads of sweat, and entered. My captain sat at the table and did not bother to turn around. He was surrounded by maps on every side. On one of them lay a pair of eyeglasses. A second pair he wore. I have never been able to make up my mind whether I like him or hate him. Watching him once during target practice, I saw him remove his glasses, and noticed that there was sadness in his eyes. Ever since then he has risen in my esteem. Now he continued to bend over the table, still without turning around. Like the Roman god Janus, he had two faces. Bristling with tiny hairs and unaware of the future, the expressionless face of his neck looked toward me, while the face which had eyes and a nose looked toward the map. It is my belief that if there is an end to this universe and if there is a God, there is also a gigantic neck, the face of which looks out toward the space beyond and is never seen. The captain's neck said to me:

"Sit down, sit down. I'll be with you in a minute."

"I left my wife in the sandbox."

"You did well."

"By the monkey bars and the slide. The tea will get cold."

"Come have a look at the photograph."

I came closer but saw nothing. I held the dark paper up against the evening light and saw that it was an X-ray. They had taken an X-ray of the entire location and of the hill. A strange bone had gotten into it, however, and I saw all my sadness and the negative of my white wife sitting in the sandbox beneath the clothesline. A breeze sprang up and papers rustled and fell to the floor. Tea was brought, and I placed my glass upon the map. "The tea is exactly over the objective," said my captain. "The point we have to capture is underneath your glass."

Afterward he entrusted me with a list of the names of those who had to be assembled. "You have to tell them when to leave their homes. Synchronize your watch with mine. You have to begin everything from the end. In reverse. But to return to the present moment, perhaps one should draw up the battle order to cover the past too, as far back as kindergarten: the attack, the final preparations, the goodbye to the wife, the last kiss, inspection of the boots, the next to the last goodbye; hopes and delusions; 'relative' peace, marriage, study, a course in communications and breaking of communications, a course in love and disappointment, father dies in the night, school, kindergarten; there you have your battle order and the calendar in reverse," laughed my captain. We stood by the window, and he rested his arm on my shoulder. "In retrospect, in retrospect," he said. . .

I went to the buffet; my wife sat in the corner over a glass of yellow juice, a straw in her mouth. She did not drink; rather, the glass seemed to drink her. As on those moonlit nights when she grows diffuse and becomes sad and empty and cannot sleep, I held on to the back of her hands, which held on to the cold glass. The small, lithe girls, wriggling in their dresses behind the counter, signalled to me that they wished to close the room for the night. The room will be closed. The world will be closed. The buffet will grow dark; the world will grow dark. As soon as my wife fell asleep I rose to my feet and left. From here on we shall grow accustomed to strange goodbyes. By the glass, by the white pillow, by the door and by all the other strange places. They are lucky, these soldiers who are shipped across the great sea; the awful ripping of paper in every goodbye is swallowed by the tremulous onrush of the waves. Here a great noise is needed to still the voice of my wife in the house next door, behind the front line. My life has always been either the noise before the stillness or the stillness before the noise. Between them I can get no rest. Will it be noisy or still, I wonder, when death comes to take me? . . .

The company clerk came and handed me the mobilization slips, as if it were a lottery. I went about the city, waking my friends so that they might gird themselves for battle. It was not always easy to do this by myself. Later I lost a number of my men. I distributed the white slips. Some were crammed through cracks in the doors like whispering snakes. Children babbled in their sleep. I answered them wakefully and they lapsed into silence. Cars cruised quietly by, secretly sliding around corners. Grown men cried. The eucalyptus tree had insomnia; it shook all over.

Each leaf was an open, smarting eye. One day, when there is peace, I shall place a eucalyptus branch where my heavy heart now lies. I stretched my hand into no-man's-land and touched a piece of paper thrown by the enemy. A midnight wind blew through the fragments of bottles. To confuse the enemy I sped to the other end of town. A woman stood in a doorway in a vacant lot and said, "He's not home, he's not home!" I heard the water being flushed in the bathroom; her husband emerged drunk with sleep, following after me as in the tale of the golden goose: whoever touches its feathers is caught fast, and must go along with it, no matter what.

I turned off my flashlight; the beam returned like a well-trained dog. We descended to the cellar, where the smell of poverty and children's sleep greeted my nostrils. But my friend was already standing before me in uniform, his pack slung over his shoulder. "What do you have in that pack?" "I don't know." His forehead was pale and deeply lined, like stairs which have been walked on a great deal. His wife stood behind me dressed in a billowy white robe. "Don't mind her," he said. She is dying already, and every evening at midnight she will appear to him. The woman faded from sight, and in her place came the steps, as white as she had been.

The roosters cry all through the night, not only at dawn. I cannot sleep the whole night long and during the day I dream. Dreams hovered above the city like vapor from a hot drink. Water flowed through every drainpipe on every roof. A single car shot off in several directions. Like my head: only my mouth remained stationary and refused to run about as did the other parts of my face. Men received instructions like police cars and shifted direction. I slipped away from the soldiers who were rounding up the company, and went off to the buffet to fetch my wife. I woke the

BATTLE FOR THE HILL
—9—

officer on duty. Sleeping soldiers littered the lawns and footpaths. I opened the door of the buffet. My wife was slumped over a tabletop, sticky with old candy, still gripping her glass. I picked her up, the glass clutched in her hand. Light struck it and it shimmered. On the way out my wife slipped from my grasp and fell, breaking the glass. My wife banged her head. She didn't even groan, and I became frightened. We sat together by the roadside. You could hear the frog-talk over the wireless in the radio car. I carried my wife home and put her to bed.

"Did you pick up the broken glass?"

"I picked it up and now I have to go."

"Why? Where to?"

"I took it you knew."

"Once you said 'I take you to be my wedded wife,' and we broke a glass then too."

"Once we sat by a white wall with vines on it."

"My head hurts."

"Because you fell. Soon it will be dawn. Do you hear a car?"

"Yes."

"They're coming for me."

"No, it's the milkman."

"No, it's the army car that's coming for me."

I packed my shirts and a few pairs of underwear. The time I had allotted to myself was up. The vehicle which passed was not the milk truck, and it was not for me. I took my belongings. When I opened my neatly pressed white handkerchief to wipe my brow, I saw that printed upon it was a plan of the enemy hill: a lonely tumbledown shack, and next to it a number of well-fortified positions. My name was embroidered below: the first initials of my name in the corner of the handkerchief which bore the plan. The approaches were indicated by arrows, the artillery emplacement by crosses or circles. I folded the handkerchief without wiping my brow. I saw that my wife was sleeping. I saw the pieces of broken glass in the street and went out. On the stairway, I switched on the light to look at the handkerchief again. What was the hill called? From where would we attack? How would we set up the light machine guns, and where would we evacuate the wounded and through what conduit in the world would all the blood flow? The long-destined hill. The ultimate hill. I have heard that the sun rises in the East. I heard the first pedestrians in the streets and I hoped that my wife would sleep on and on. I folded the handkerchief lovingly and put it away. I drank a cup of coffee standing up, without sensing the taste of war. New death notices had been put up on the bulletin board. There were also posters calling on the residents of different cities to assemble for memorial rallies in honor of the Six Million. In all probability these were mobilization calls in disguise. The newspaper fell from my hands and I let it lie.

A car drove up and stopped near me: "Come with me." "Where are you going? You're not from the army?" The driver laughed and said, "Don't you see the way I've smeared the windshields with mud?" The earth is rising. The fragrance of the earth is rising. He then showed me pictures of his children. "Where are we going?" He held his hand up before my eyes and said, "Here is the map, we will follow the lines on my palm." The water sloshed about in his canteen. "Soon we will be home again," I said to calm him. Like my mother, who used to calm us by saying about everything that it was nothing. If it was blistering hot she said, "Just another summer day." When it hailed she said, "How pleasant the air is, so mild and fresh! It's good that it's not too dry. It's good there is no drought."

The strings from which I dangled like a marionette in

a puppet show became entwined and tangled among other strings; when somebody else was supposed to move I moved instead, and vice versa. And all the time the voice fixed above our heads continued to talk. I asked the driver to stop, and I went to call one of the men in my company who lived in a large courtyard; the passageway was still sealed off with the branches of trees that had broken during the winter. Over the door was a sheet of paper with the names of all the tenants. Next to each name was written how many times to ring. I rang four times. I waited, but the door did not open. I watched the open army trucks pass by, decked out with the long hair of girls, with antennas and machine guns. Although I knew that there was still time, I hid behind the door. I heard footsteps approaching. The door opened. A man saw me and turned pale; he then returned to his room to put on his glasses. Then he begged my pardon for the delay in opening the door; he didn"t know if it was ringing for him. Sometimes it rings four times and it's not for him. During his vacations he lies on his back and counts the number of rings. He is always waiting. He has often been mistaken. He has often been mistaken in his life. He is a teacher and there are stacks of notebooks in his room, filled with red marks correcting students' mistakes. Like his life. In his room is a single window, and the blinds are generally lowered. He finished arranging his things and came with me. Civilian cars which had been commandeered for the war passed by, camouflaged with mud and dark blankets.

Toward evening I was assigned to observe the hill with the shack for the first time. I entered a house which stood near the border. The stairway was empty and the plaster was peeling from the walls, on which a few mailboxes hung. In one box the letters overflowed. The tenant was long gone, but the letters continued to arrive. Sometimes, when I have wandered far in my thoughts, people speak to me and their words clutter the gateways to my being without penetrating any further, because I do not choose to admit them.

I went up to the top floor. A woman wiping her hands on an apron let me in. I showed her the letter from the army. Domestic odors permeated the house. A pressure burner chattered noisily. A girl sang in the bathtub and soap bubbles popped all over her—but I was unable to see. My heart welled up within me, and all the words which had accumulated in my head like letters in the abandoned mailbox suddenly fell and glutted my heart instead. I recalled my mission and my eyes grew bleary with worry, like the camouflaged windshields which were smeared with mud. A boy stood and stared at me. I formed an arch over him like the vault of the skies; the worries smudged my eyes. The boy's mouth was smudged with food. I ascended to the attic. I lay down between the wooden crates with the boy at my feet. "What are you looking at?" he asked. "At the years to come," I answered, "and at my wife lying in bed because her head is broken." The boy left; I heard his laugh from a distance. My captain was already at the window. The wire screen was in our way. We ripped it apart and were deluged by dust. My captain passed me the binoculars.

"Do you see that ridge? Do you see that line, that elevation, that trench, that point?" I saw them, and we compared them with the map. The world was exact and efficient. My captain got up to go. "Stay a while," he said to me, "and take notes on whatever you see." I took notes: A man went by with his donkey. A man went by with his wife. The sun is slowly setting. A man is stretching himself by the shack and lifting his two arms. To whom is he surrendering?

I heard footsteps behind me. The boy returned and

began to ask questions. I gave him pencil and paper and told him to draw the hill. He drew the hill with himself standing on it. He drew a flag and a ball rolling down the slope. More officers arrived to take their first glimpse of the lonely outpost. I returned by way of the apartment. The bathroom door was open and the burner had stopped chattering. I asked permission to wash my hands. The girl whose voice I had heard before stood in front of me. "Why are you staring at me like a dummy?" she said. "Help me dry my back!" I took the towel and massaged her skin until it turned red.

"What did you do up there in the attic?" she asked.

"We looked."

"Did you see my old dolls?"

"I'll come back."

"My back is already dry. Now on your way!"

She laughed, tossing her thick black hair. Her eyes sparkled and her mouth was red. Drops of water from her hair fell onto my khaki shirt and dried instantly. Her snub nose was fresh and provoking. She caught me by the ears and said, "You're coming back, you're coming back to me!" After seeing her, I couldn't go straight back to the army, so I took a roundabout route by way of the valleys which encircle the city. The Spanish consul drove past in his automobile. The consul of chaos hoisted his ensign. Jews gathered in the Orthodox quarter of Mea Shearim to cry Ma'ariv Ma'ariv,* their faces turned toward an east which is no longer the East. East is the magnetic pole of the Jews. I glanced at my watch and saw that it was time to be in the school building for the parents' meeting; I sat in the teachers' lounge and waited for the parents to arrive. What-

---

*Ma'ariv is the Jewish daily evening prayer. Literally, the word means "evening," and is related to the word ma'arav, which means "west."

ever way you look at it, there is no helping the parents and no preventing bloodshed on the hill with the shack. Only time can occasionally intervene and permit life to linger on a little longer. Bergman stuck his head in the door to see if I had come. One of his children is alive and the other is dead. The dead child is lobbying for him in the world to come. He has already made inroads among the dead; he is an honorary consul in heaven. The child who is still living studies with me. Bergman was with me in the army during the Second World War. Now he sat silently before me. In the glass cabinet there stood the physics apparatus: pieces that interlock, for example, though we never interlock; or the lead ball, which after being heated cannot pass through the ring because it no longer fits. There were also shells from Elath in which you could listen to the sea, and a paper world glued to a globe, very like the world glued to the head on my shoulders, which is also nearly round.

The sister of one of my pupils approached me; she was already grown up and married. One of her eyes she fixed on me; the other was blind and white, with the eyeball turned inward. Aging fathers came who failed to recognize their own sons: "Which one do you mean, which one do you mean, Yosef or Shmuel?" Fathers resemble their sons and everybody resembles everybody, and we are all enemies nonetheless. I placed the plan of the hill beside my grade book, and from time to time I peeked at it. Beneath the grades for discipline, for good behavior and arithmetic, were the dotted lines which stood for the enemy positions. I had been informed that my company was not to be held responsible for capturing the entire hill, but only for its southern slope. Beyond that there remained a few dirt embankments, and a handful of enemy soldiers sitting behind them. When we really attack it will not be necessary to pin numbers on our backs like basketball players to avoid mistaking one side for the other; we won't make mistakes. And if we do, that too is ultimately no mistake. In the meantime much was happening: The sun set. Children screamed. A wind blew. Dust came and the window was shut. As in the Book of Job, one messenger was followed by another. The teacher, Miss Ziva, had arrived.

"We're on to you, we know all about you."

I covered the plan with my hand so that Ziva should not see it. It was forbidden for security reasons.

"We know all about you, all about the girl whose back you wiped."

Miss Ziva has read widely and is an expert on weather conditions and the heavenly winds. She is prettier in winter than in summer. Someone's father stepped forward and complained that his son was noisy and unruly, that he colored the walls of the house all the colors of the sunset, that he threw stones at cats and dogs and was spoiling his mother's dreams.

Miss Ziva was irritated. "Why don't you give them some advice?" Her eyes are as hard as metal screws. Once she wanted to rivet herself to the world with those eyes, but she didn't succeed. Once we went for a walk in the fields, her nylon stockings ripped on a thornbush, and she became angry with me. To this day she traverses the world with those hard blue eyes. Why had she come to me?

I was being called from the street. "Wait just a minute," I said, "one more mother." "I can't begin to tell you," said the mother when she came, "what a nuisance my naughty girl has been to me ever since she lay in my belly."

Bergman went off to an adjoining room to chat with the other teachers. The shadows under his eyes were like the shadows cast by a cloud that refuses to pass. His wife must say to him, "You have to get ahead in the world!" So he gets ahead, but the cloud beneath his eyes recalls him to the starting point. Bergman is a surveyor; what does he do? He goes out every morning and plants his black and white rods deep in the waste and, gazing into the distance like a prophet: here will be houses, here will be gardens and cemeteries! I, on the other hand, have to prophesy about the men who will live in these houses. He always has his queer equipment about him. His poles, his theodolite, his scrolls, his registers, his calculations.

Bergman unbuttoned his overcoat to show me how his lapel was torn like a mourner's. Then he unbuttoned his shirt and took out his undershirt. I saw that even his chest bore the print of dried mud, just like the transports. "You see," he said to me, "I too." Men used to sprinkle ashes on their heads as a sign of mourning; now they cake themselves with earth because of the war. Bergman rearranged his clothing and left me with the globe, whose surface had peeled away with the years. A compass and a ruler hung from a hook: these delude the children no less than the teachers, because they foster the illusion that there is really such a thing as a straight line and a pure angle. The picture of the living President stared at the picture of the dead President. The picture of Bialik hung aslant and I straightened it. My favorite pupil entered the room. I patted her on the cheek, smudging her complexion with earth, like Bergman's chest and the cars. "What fun it will be," she said to me happily, "now I too can go to your war!"

When I left, it was already night and my wife was waiting for me at the bottom of the stairs. How did she know I was here? Her hair rustled and the briars rustled and there was a smell of burning in the air and her eyes grew black like after the Great Fire. "Come," I said to her, "we will go wake up some men so that the army may be brought up to full strength." The first person on our list was a milkman, whose hallway smelt of milk. We entered the courtyard; there are no longer many like it in Jerusalem. By the entrance there once lived an old professor from Czechoslovakia who came here with the escaping Czech army. How he came to be a professor and how he arrived here with the army, I don't know. He lived in a decrepit structure which had one wall adjacent to a ceramics kiln. He was always worrying that this house might go up in flames. He was feeble and emaciated like a dwarf, and though he dwelt above the ground, he lived, as dwarfs do, in the subterranean caverns of his soul. His voice was high and quavering like that of a mouse. Besides him, there lived in the old house an ancient bookbinder, whose sons were scattered about the world. While they drifted over the face of the earth as if swept by gusts of wind, he stuck to his post and fussily tended his books. His two youngest sons were arrested by the British police at the door of his bindery for illegal possession of weapons. The owner of the house was an Armenian doctor who lived in the Old City. Tall, thin and sharp-featured, he put in an appearance every now and then. There was also a storage bin for green vegetables, and sacks of peanuts and more vegetables were piled in a small courtyard.

One room was always rented to independent young girls, the kind who come to Jerusalem to study at the Music Conservatory or at the Bezalel Art School, and take up rug weaving or work in ceramics. They are always independent. When it suits their mood they have a gentleman caller, and when it suits their mood otherwise they kick him out through the courtyard. All day long they are always laundering something. On the top floor was a small school for little girls: the floorboards above the rooms creak with footsteps all day and sharp screams punctuate the recesses. Once I sat in one of those rooms and held an eight-day-old baby on my knees, held him forcibly because he was being circumcised. Afterward there were little cakes and neighbors, and the wine flowed forlornly into the guests and into that sea which is the receptacle for everything.

My friend the soldier, whom I wished to remind of his military duty, sat by the potter's wheel. He was a potter and worked with clay. Behold the potter in the hands of his clay, I thought to myself. I reversed all the proverbs I knew, and I saw that nothing ever changed in this world. You can bury the living and quicken the dead and nothing will change. "Wait a moment," said the soldier, "I want to finish this pitcher." The shelves along the wall were lined with scores of pitchers waiting to dry. Much time and much quiet ripening is needed for anything to be finished and perfect. In wartime, however, the unfinished is taken along with the finished, the dry with the wet. Boys are promoted to the rank of adults and ripen too quickly. Whoever breaks, breaks, and those who return no longer have the patience to sit and await their turn like those pitchers. They want to be useful and functional right away. They want a coat of glaze before they are even dry. Later, when the cracks begin to appear, they will be irreparable.

The potter took his rifle from underneath his bed and began to clean it: the barrel and the breechblock and the two sights, far and near. I have seen many sights in my life. I told him where to go and departed. I waited at the bus stop with my wife. The bus came and she got on. The doors shut and she reached for her fare. She handed the driver a large bill and he had to stop his vehicle and give her change. All her life she has paid for everything with large bills. She sat by the window, resting her head against the back of the seat. The bus lurched forward and disappeared, and she shouted something at me from the window which I couldn't make out. Her speech is like a patch of cloud. When will the rain come? I was overcome by a terrible fear that soon I would be lying mangled and in need of patching on the field adjoining the hill.

I decided to go to the observation post to see the hill by night. I came to the house. A bicycle leaned against the door. Whose was it? The girl stood in the doorway and said, "I knew you would come."

"Perhaps you want your back wiped?"

"You have a dirty mind. Have you got a cigarette?"

"I don't smoke. What are you trying to do to me?"

"I'm not doing anything to you."

"Why are you wearing a red skirt?"

I tried to get past but she wouldn't let me: Don't look at your hill, look at me! I forced my way and she clung to me. I broke free and manacled her with the bicycle lock. "Don't go away," I said, "don't go. Soon I'll be down again." I climbed the stairs to another apartment which was unoccupied and bored through the wall until I could see. The hill was bathed in moonlight. I saw shadowy men shovelling earth like gravediggers; the sound of metal striking against stone reverberated through the air. I added some lines and semicircles to my map, while on a separate slip of paper I wrote: assembly point, evacuation route, two machine guns, preliminary range finding, searchlights, ammunition crates in the small yard. I jotted down a few more notes in the same fashion. When I came downstairs the girl was still standing there, but the bicycle chain was broken. She doesn't know that all will be destroyed.

"Even though I broke loose, I waited for you." She stood like a heavy white cloud in the darkness.

"There isn't a chance in the world," I said to her.

"What are those clouds for?"

"The Nile is overflowing its banks."

"The Nile overflows its banks every year. Why don't you have any children? I'd come and be their nurse." She kept me company to the top of the street, where we were stopped by a soldier hiding in a bread truck. I gave the password and we went on. Afterward, I walked her home, and we stood on either side of the clothesline. Her black sleeveless dress had been hung up to dry. It was inside-out, and she stood beside it very sure of herself.

"How old are you?"

"Seventeen."

"Such a big girl, and your navel hasn't even healed yet."

"Silly boy, would you like to take a look?"

"Your navel has healed, but your eyes have not healed. After the separation your eyes will never heal. Once you were in the womb of the world. When you came forth and they cut your cord you were separated, and were no longer part of it. That's why you long for it, and your eyes have not healed." She laughed and fended me off with her hand: "Go on, go on, you and your maps and your plans." "It's because the plans are as sad as my face," I said to her. "Your face, my dear, has no sadness and no plans and is unprepared for the future."

A sergeant passed by. "Walk along with me," he said, "I have to get my army boots." His army boots were in storage where his old father and mother live. He himself is married and has children and a home of his own, but he leaves his army boots with his parents. His old mother brought him a ladder. He went up to the attic and disappeared there to search. His mother looked at me. "Why are they calling you?" she asked. I shrugged my shoulders.

That night signs of the impending battle multiplied in the blacked-out city. Cars drove through the streets at a whisper, children ceased to shout. My wife took in the wash from the roof; women soldiers dressed in pajamas stood by the antennas and spoke into space. Work tools were readied in the cemeteries, and secret arsenals were opened in grocery stores and beneath monuments and sleeping men. Outdoors, human chains passed crates from hand to hand in the square. Jews maddened by the Psalms stood in courtyards, trumpeters and drummers practiced in the youth centers. Proclamations were pasted to human backs. Rams' horns were tested, and new machinery and freshly lubricated hopes were brought out into the open. Arms were cached underground. Hearts were tested. Soldiers rested beneath their blankets in driveways, like candleless dead. Queues formed before the cinemas; men picked each other clean of memories, like old notices stripped from a bulletin board, in order to be ready and not weighed down by past events. At the entrance to the city, each citizen received the Insignia of the Holy Earth. Man and his engines preserve Thou, O Lord! Ambulances drove by masked with flapping nets, like the veils on the Bride of Death. Women blessed the Sabbath candles though it was only a weekday. Girls in hoop skirts parachuted in the public squares. Metallic sounds filled the air. Commands were whispered. Loudspeakers were set up. Silent speakers frightened the sleepers.

The following day kindergarten children were driven to the border and told to dance and play for the sake of camouflage. Young girls were brought and told to wear colorful clothing with bright buttons for the sake of camouflage. In the evening pairs of lovers were transported and told to make love before the enemy's eyes for the sake of camouflage, so that the enemy might not see the preparations for the terrible battle.

My captain came and said, "We have to find another house from which we can see the southern side of the hill." We circled the hill like Balaam and Balak. "Just a minute," I said, "just a minute." My wife's hand was firmly in my own. Big hands must hold little hands: this is their duty in the world. My wife looked at my captain with hostility. "I too have left my wife and children," he said. My captain showed us pictures of his wife and children. They smiled the way people smile on the pictures you find in the pockets of dead soldiers. We approached the sentry, who was our grocer but was now guarding the way. "Your wife can go no farther," he said; "from here on the front begins." He gave her a jar of yogurt, some plum jelly and a few other provisions, and she went home. She was too weighed down to turn around, but I watched her go. It was well that she had her hands full with the jars she was carrying. From here on I was deeply engrossed in conversation with my captain.

"They've added four new positions during the night."

"And they've added rolls of barbed wire there, a whole sea of barbed wire, and mines near the red house in the southern valley."

"This will be our assembly point. It has water, drainage and sewerage. It has an exit and an entrance to the world."

"Where will we set up the machine guns?"

"Many will fall."

A Yemenite boy came along and we bought two sticks of ice cream from him. We sucked them until only the sticks were left. We took the sticks and traced out a map on the ground, pointing with them as one does with the pointer of a Torah scroll. More officers joined the conference. They all scratched lines and dots in the ground, manipulating little stones and bigger stones. I pretended I was going to urinate and left the circle. As soon as I gained the nearest corner I began to run, stopping only when I had reached home. My wife was not there, so I stood by the window. Now that I was preparing to leave again, I noticed for the first time the trees in the garden beyond the wall. A breeze stirred them, and they swayed as if in the act of love. Our wall touched the next wall. The next wall nudged the next house with its shoulder, as if to pass on the news. Were I King Solomon, I would know what they were saying about the coming battle. I lowered my head. My head was like a flag at half-mast. Only then did I spy the slip of paper, left for me by my wife on the coffee table:

"I'm at Mother's, come."

I marvelled that the slip should be faded and yellow like a Dead Sea Scroll, for the note had been written only today and the paper had been white and fresh. Under the kites flown by the children, I skirted the city. In a nook where I had once made love, by the very rock, a sentry sat cooking himself a meal. He pointed at the kites in the sky and at the charred trunks of the olive trees. He pointed because his mouth was busy chewing. At his side lay a compass in which a needle nervously revolved. A boy ran after a dog which he held on a leash. What were they chasing, who chased them? A cannon stood in readiness beneath a latticework of thorns. I approached my mother's house from the valley, so that she had no advance warning. The road was inscribed with chalk arrows, all pointing in the same direction, as in a children's game. I practically followed them all the way. The quarter in which my mother lives is a small one, and is inhabited by artists and students and lofty trees and Yemenites and Germans and old settlers of Jerusalem who work in the foundations and the labor federation. Often when I am leaving the area on Saturday nights, I see crowds of people climbing the steps which lead into it. A young couple, pressed against each other; two girls, one pretty and the other with muscle-bound legs, returning from their youth center. The neighborhood swallows them all. A young man pushes a perambulator up the steps and his wife carries the baby. Dogs and cats. Even the letter carrier who brings the mail. I have seen him only entering the neighborhood, never leaving it—as if it refused to let him go. The same for the milkman, and another pair of lovers, who stroll side by side touching palms. Somebody is always playing the piano in my mother's neighborhood. Sometimes the late sonatas of Beethoven, sometimes the early sonatas of first love. The neighborhood swallows them all, and is never too full and never short of space. They never build new houses in it, or add new stories to the old ones. Many of the apartments can be reached only by means of winding, open-air staircases. There is even a small public park, planted in honor of a soldier, a neighborhood boy, who was killed. His father comes daily to water the trees. He leans over to water them with love, and the trees grow straight and their leaves are shiny. Sometimes the girl who plays the piano places a sprig of glossy eucalyptus leaves where her heart is. When her boyfriend comes home from the army he kneads the leaves, and the pungent smell reaches his nose. The neighborhood slopes toward the valley. Women set out their laundry and boys send up their kites, and all find their way to heaven.

I asked my mother for some sacks which might be filled with sand and used for protection against bombardment. My mother's attic is spacious, and full of old costumes for Purim masquerades. She took the pouch which held my father's prayer shawl, filled it with sand and sewed old clothes together into additional sacks—all because it was an emergency. I ate standing up. My wife was not there and came only at the last minute. She went with me to the assembly point. I noticed that the garden wall was caving in, that the well was empty, and that the trenches by the roadside gaped as wide as ever. We walked through the narrow alleyways; it was afternoon and the streets were clear. A soldier stood on top of a high building, signalling with flags to a distant place. I signalled to myself inwardly, to my blood, which was sufficiently alarmed as it was. My sister stood in a telephone booth, placing a call. She could not let go of the receiver, but she gesticulated at me with her head. While her mouth talked into the distance, her eyes conversed with me. We have always had good times together, and now perhaps I am going to meet my death. When we were children we divided the world between us. Even when we were angry with each other and came to blows, we fought wisely and with a plan; I would turn my back to her and let her beat me with clenched fists without resisting. Then it would be my turn to beat her, and she would sit and not interfere. With that, the quarrel was over. Though we disagreed, we never enjoyed the blows, and our ears were insensitive to that wonderfully resonant drum, the pummelled body.

We reached the designated corner. My captain was waiting with some other members of the company. The truck was due in three minutes. My captain was angry because I had run away. He removed his eyeglasses, so as not to see the tears in the eyes of the women. I deposited the bag of candies on the ground; the paper was beginning to rip, and the colored wrappers sparkled. The truck arrived, covered with drying mud. The motor started. "It begins tonight," whispered my captain into my ear. I knew that I would never see my wife again. It was a winter day, but her face was as dry as if it had been parched by a sirocco. She didn't want to cry but the tears came. Her whole body shared them, her hands and her legs, her hair and her thighs, until her torso became heavy and only her face remained dry. When we began to move it was like an eclipse of the moon. The side of the house encroached upon her fine, round face. Slowly the wall surged forward, until her face was completely covered. As she walked home she rocked back and forth a little. Her blood cried like an infant. She had to calm it. Her body was like a cradle for her blood, but the more she rocked it the harder it cried.

The truck jolted on and we rocked in it like drunkards. "It's apparently scheduled for tonight," said my captain, "but I'm not entirely sure. We'll have to billet the company." We found a house still in the process of construction. Part of it lay buried beneath wooden planks; the ceiling was dripping, for the concrete had only been poured the day before and a series of posts held it in place. We started to change our clothing: short pants for long, and long for short. The men scattered through the building. The rooms, which were not quite finished, rang with their voices. The practical jokers went about saying: This is the bathroom. This is the tub. I'm a gorgeous lady, soaping herself naked.

We sat upon sacks of cement near some barrels of whitewash, watching the patchy sky through blank windows. The night passed in a steady medley of men alighting from trucks and the clomp of boots, doors slamming, and heavy utensils falling angrily. We lay in a small, empty room. The runner lay down at our feet. By his side were the machine gun, the ram's horn, and the evening paper. We were awakened frequently during the night by the arrival of reinforcements: shadowy men stood outside like beggars, waiting for us to find them a place and distribute arms. My captain got up in the middle of the night and left. When he returned, he proceeded to shine his flashlight on the sleeping men. He held a fresh packet of papers in his hand, like a bouquet— collections of orders. We got up and took our bearings anew; the enemy had strengthened the hill. There were cannon and minefields and women crying in village doorways. Some of the mines were exploding already, through mental telepathy. We were forced to revise the entire assault.

We crisscrossed the city, distributing ammunition.

BATTLE FOR THE HILL

Everybody received a package. We hid ammunition in milk buckets, in toyboxes, and underneath our hats, so that the enemy would not know where it was. In the morning, when we went to observe the hilltop, we saw that a change had come over it—like a body covered with freckles, it was arrayed with redoubts and fresh trenches. There were no shadows, and the wind piled the clouds in a high bank. I went to school. I meant to place a book upon the table, but instead I put down some bullets and an empty canteen. The children were wild and refused to settle down. The young teacher erased the board with her long hair and smiled at me. She was my substitute. I drew a plan of the hill on the blackboard with different colored chalk. "This is new territory," I said. "We will learn all about it." I drew arrows, dotted lines, circles, and crosses. The teacher laid her hand on my shoulder and said in a sad voice, "Calm down, relax!" I erased the board and left. I ran all the way home; it was already evening, it was night. My wife was asleep; I didn't wake her. The world was quiet, and I lay on my back. The light from the neighbors' window cast an illuminated square upon the ceiling. People drifted home from their revelling. The young couple whose wedding picture I had seen somewhere in a photographer's box returned home too. The bride's voice was husky, sweet and honeyed in its lower register. Perhaps she sings too much at parties. Doors closed—of houses, of motorcars, of people. My eyes were wide open. Trucks passed, going in different directions. This reassured me. Had they been going in the same direction it would mean that the battle was starting; since they went in different directions, they meant no harm. I debated whether to wake my wife or let her sleep. Opportunities to talk are few. Always the stillness before the noise, and always the noise before the stillness. In the noise we cannot hear one another. In the stillness we cannot talk for fear of being overheard. I lay on my stomach, taking cover behind the pillow. In my mind's eye I saw the terrible hill. That very moment the area under barbed wire was being enlarged. An ocean of barbed wire. Half the company would be mowed down. I was about to doze off when there came a knock on the door. The front bell rang. The company clerk was pale: "Come at once!" I dressed silently. The clerk had already gone ahead; he descended many steps, some of which weren't even there. My wife sat on the bed, hugging her knees close to her body, as if to say: these have remained loyal and stayed with me. I snatched a sweater from the chest of drawers. All the sweaters tumbled out, red ones and yellow ones, hers and mine. My wife sobbed like a child who has been roused from its sleep. I am going out to die. This time I said my goodbyes to her forehead, rather than to her mouth or hand. Behind the hard forehead soft thoughts dwell, and beyond where thoughts harden, soft hair.

I went downstairs. I wanted to do it quietly, but my spiked boots shattered the silence. I headed for the unfinished building. Along the narrow walled pavement, a former pupil of mine knelt to fix her shoes. I asked her why she sat there after midnight. She looked me up and down, while her hands attended to the shoes.

"How was it on the kibbutz? Didn't you go to a kibbutz after finishing your studies?"

"It was lovely, but I've been left all alone. They've all gone off to the war, and my shoes have torn."

I saw that she had grown up and would no longer listen to me. My pupils are scattered all over the world. One is already dead. I had no time to talk with the girl. She looked pretty in the beam of the flashlight. She squatted on one heel, fixing the shoe on the opposite foot. As she sat, her body seemed to fill out. Not so my thoughts, which were pointed like the prow of a ship. Why had she run away from home? I'm not going to war. The war is by my front step. The gate to my house is the beginning of the front. "I don't understand you," she said. "When I was your pupil I never understood you either; then you used to scold me. Now I'm grown up and pretty, and I sit before you in the night between two walls and my thighs are full."

A motorcyclist drove up, blinding me with his lights; he drew to a stop, and I hopped onto the back seat. The girl continued to squat on the pavement. Perhaps she saw an angel, blocking the road with drawn sword, someone I could not see. I came to the building; no one was there but the old watchman. The barrels of whitewash were where I had left them, as was the dripping from the concrete roof. A cat crossed between the watchman and me. "They left an hour ago," he said. "See, the papers are still fluttering on the spot where company headquarters was. Here is a strap that was left behind." I picked up a buckle from some piece of equipment. Where is my buckle, where does my life fasten? The buckle is death. It fits practically any strap. I threw the buckle away and wandered through the city, searching for my company. An engineering unit was throwing a temporary iron bridge across the square. I asked why they were building it but received no answer. A lone cannon rolled silently down the street on rubber wheels, until it ran into a telephone pole and came to a halt. An overturned car lay at the intersection, its wheels still spinning in the air. A pair of lovers came by and crawled into the car, sitting there upside-down while the wheels turned above them. I remembered a soldier in my unit who lived in an abandoned British army base. In order to get there I had to cut across an alleyway. "So you've forgiven me, have you?" cried a voice from the cellar. Bending over, I caught sight of Nissim; myopic Nissim with the thick lenses, who was forever breaking his glasses and having to get a new pair made. He had never learned to fire a rifle, and we hadn't bothered to call him. He left the cellar, however, tagging along behind me until we reached the deserted base. Nothing was left of it but a couple of old stoves, a few ramshackle bungalows and an outhouse. Many things were scrawled on the walls of the outhouse: *Out of bounds! Officers only! For children! Auxiliary corps for women only!* Over these was written in Hebrew: *Men. Ladies. Company D. Yoska is an ass. Down with German rearmament! General John, go home! For shame! Up with Spanish rearmament!*

I stood beneath the sign which said *Out of bounds,* but I was definitely within bounds. Bounded by death and by destiny. I saw the soldier I had been looking for sitting amongst some ruins, reading a book. His beard was short and fluffy, and he had a face like Jesus. When I seized him he said, "I still haven't caught up on my sleep from the last mobilization. I need a great deal of sleep to nourish my thoughts." I sent Nissim to have his glasses repaired because they broke. I was left with the soldier who resembled Jesus. The wire fence was like the crown of thorns placed around his head. A truck came by and we were handed a spool of telephone wires. The two of us grabbed a pole, and passing it through the cylinder we began to walk. There were many kinds of wire, in several colors. Wires for good news and for bad news, and wires for whispered longings, such as: Where are you?

> I'm forbidden to say.
> Raise your voice.
> It's forbidden to raise it.
> Raise your head.
> It's raised.
> I wish I could see you.

BATTLE FOR THE HILL

I'm like the receiver in your hands: ears to speak with and a mouth to listen.

We walked and walked until the wire ran out. We put down the empty metal spool. Children came and played with it, rolling it about. Girls jumped rope with the colored wires. We passed on, treading on the chalk lines drawn by the children. The game the children play is not to step on the lines, but to jump over them. We stepped on them. God, or somebody like Him, does the same to us—as soon as we draw up rules and lines and boundaries, He comes with his monstrous feet and steps on them, because He doesn't care.

We came to a courtyard by the edge of the city which had an observation post. Every point in Jerusalem is a beachhead but everything is dry and there is no ocean of water. Yet the sea of Jerusalem is the most terrible sea of all. Every place in Jerusalem is a tongue of the city—and the city has many tongues and nobody understands her. I have tried many times to cut my ties with Jerusalem, and each time I have remained. If I come back safe and sound from the battle on the hill, I shall never return to Jerusalem!

I walked on, and as I walked I thought, a thinking man walking along a street always looks beaten. A man walking in a khaki uniform is better off not thinking. One day they will arrest him and call him a traitor and demand to know his thoughts. My thoughts finally brought me to a narrow valley; my company was camped beneath the olive trees. I had not even had time to sit down before I was besieged with requests for passes. I had to give every man an answer, and no man was dispensable.

He said, "I'm a storekeeper, the margarine is streaming through the cracks in the door."

I answered him, "My longings for my wife are also streaming."

He said, "I haven't received my pay yet."

I answered, "Your children will collect your pay for you."

He said, "They won't give it to them without my signature."

I answered, "I have my signature and I still don't know who I am."

He said, "It's the anniversary of my father's death, I want to recite the mourner's prayer."

I answered, "We are all dying, and the clouds will rain upon us, and there's no need to pray."

Hours passed, and I grew weary. Doctors and nurses came to examine our blood; a nurse jabbed her needle into a stray vein. A doctor saw the blood and said, "It's no good."

All the officers who were to take part in the attack gathered together. Artillery experts came to coordinate the shelling, chaplains to coordinate the aid of Providence, and every now and then somebody brought his wife. "It's good for the women to see that it's not so terrible," said our captain. Once more we attacked the hill and made calculations. Man and his guns preserve Thou, O Lord! Information arrived which put an entirely different slant on things: what we had thought to be barbed wire was really men, and what we had thought to be bunkers were gun emplacements. Once more nothing was certain. Death alone was certain for all. I revised the map according to the latest information. My ink ran out. I borrowed a pen from my wife. The pen fell between the ammunition crates, on which were written: *Fragile—Handle with Care, No Smoking—Explosive Material, Keep in a Cool Dark Place.* I too wanted to lie down in a cool dark place, and write *Handle with Care* on myself. I never found the pen, but the panic I experienced on the first night failed to return. Sometimes a great clarity strikes me flush between the eyes. Autumn days come, cleansing the troubled winds of summer. A group of soldiers crouched by a dip in the valley and played *Questions and Answers*. I knew that on the following evening they would be asking no questions, but would be lying in wait for the zero hour. Among a patrol of riflemen I met my little pupil Mazal, who is seven years old. She has large eyes, her mother is a slut, and her father is an Arak drinker. "I'm going off to the war with you," she said. "I'm a nurse, and I have a white cap and a white apron left over from Purim."

"You have to go home. Your mother will worry."

"She won't worry."

"And your little brothers?"

"I've already taken care of them and fixed them some food."

"It's not Purim now. You have to go to school."

"They don't let me go because I have lice in my hair. The teacher made me leave."

"Rinse your hair with kerosene and have it cut!"

She shook her black curls. "I won't cut it, I'm going to war with you. If I cut it I won't be strong. Didn't we learn about Samson?"

"But a little girl like you has to keep clean," I told her.

She threw me a long look which travelled from one end of Jerusalem to the other. I sat her down in the playground, which had been converted into the evacuation center for the wounded. She started to play with the dolls. She listened to their heartbeats and gave them injections. One of the dolls was exuding dry seaweed and she bandaged it. Chairs scraped overhead; I could tell that the staff meeting was over. I heard men jumping into trucks, the clank of metal, and meters turning over. My captain came in and saw Mazal, but said nothing; he waved the bundle of papers in his hand. I grabbed hold of Mazal and we climbed together to the attic. We could see the hill. "Your eyes are tired," she said, "let me look." I gave her the binoculars.

"What do you see, Mazal?"

"Men standing and passing green crates."

"What else?"

"Many sacks, and barbed wire like a lot of curls."

"What else?"

"Now they're hiding. All I see is bushes and mounds of dirt."

I came down with Mazal from the observation post and asked my wife to take her home. They linked hands and disappeared. Everything is always disappearing, and I can retain nothing. "Where is the young girl?" I asked the tenants, "the one who sings in the bathtub?" She had gone to a party for the American Marines who work at the consulate. I stood in the doorway. Tracers lit the night, but the eternal light within my brain flickered silently and feebly. I went to the American building. A row of colored bottles stood against the wall. I watched the girl dance; her crinolines flapped about her waist, a red crinoline and a black one and a white one. She didn't notice me. She only stopped dancing when her thighs grew chilly. The American Marines laughed, and she joined in their laughter. The American flag rippled like waves. I stepped outside. I passed a hard wall. I wanted to press myself against the terrible wall of history, like Rashi's mother.* I wanted to find myself a niche safe from an intransigent History. I wanted a miracle

---

*According to an old Jewish legend, the mother of Rashi, the famous eleventh-century biblical exegete, was walking one day in a narrow, walled-in street in Worms during her pregnancy. A carriage came toward her and she was in danger of being crushed; she pressed herself against the wall behind, and the wall miraculously opened to receive her.

BATTLE FOR THE HILL

—35—

to come to pass, so I should not have to lie mutilated on the hillside.

I returned to my pup tent. I thought a lot. I heard a voice saying, "At exactly eleven-fifty-eight we begin the bombardment." I thought some more. Finally, I raised my hand and switched off my thoughts the way you switch off a bed lamp. I was awakened frequently during the night. I imagined I was being called. I fell asleep again. A cold wind blew through the valley, slicing it open like a knife gutting fish. In the morning I couldn't tell whether there had been an attack or not. We continued to observe the hill. The earth was like those Christian saints who suffer from stigmata on their hands and feet, where the nails passed through Jesus and the cross. The earth was like them, bursting open where the shells were due to fall.

We strengthened our positions. We filled sandbags, and went off with our girl friends and wives to make love. We strolled down the streets, singing and dancing. One day a soldier approached me and I asked him what unit he belonged to. "I have no unit," he answered. "What is that insignia on your shoulder?" "It's not an insignia. It's a patch. My shirt ripped." I noticed that some of his front teeth were missing. The company runner appeared, and I recalled that it was my job to see about hot drinks. I requisitioned a number of soldiers and we set off with empty buckets in our hands. We went to the large kitchen in the basement. It was not yet daybreak. Shouting to make themselves heard, the cooks moved among the lurid flames as if they were in Hell. "Where is the tea?" I shouted. The head cook pointed to a bucket. An oily, metallic, vaporous smell filled the air. We passed through the small courtyard, skidding on our boots. A fine rain began to fall. From the communications office came the laughter of the women operators. We put down our buckets and peered through the lighted windows. Even then the tea refused to calm down. All we saw in the window was the light.

That whole day the men practiced rapid mobilization. First they were told to go to work, and they went. Then the alarm was sounded, and they were made to lie in the trenches, in readiness for the attack. By evening we had reached a terrific speed of mobilization—the men threw away their work tools on the double and were handed rifles. In this manner I managed to spend part of my time in school. I appeared suddenly from behind a map of Asia Minor, frightening the children. My captain came in the night: Now it's in earnest! I looked him in the eyes.

"You're joking."

"No, this time it's serious."

The men were already asleep in their jumping-off positions. We went to take a last look. The streets were empty, and the vacant lots were hoarse as if from too much shouting. We lay down in a briar patch opposite the hill. My captain and I dozed off from time to time. In the early hours of the morning I suddenly asked, "How much longer?" He shook his head, and the bushes rustled by his shoulder. At daybreak I noticed that the bush above my head was larger than my head, and larger than the rising sun. I noticed that the dry grass beside me swayed and trembled, while the grass in the distance was tranquil. The world resembles men who are all looking around a corner at the same thing. I watch them from a distance, and cannot tell what it is they find so fascinating. We went to sit at a marble table in a small restaurant and made a complete inventory: the delivery of weapons after the hill was taken and the evacuation of the wounded. We heard the clanking of metal. My captain jumped to his feet and shouted, "The tanks are coming!" We saw there were no tanks, only a truck piled high with bottles. We laughed. Rather than look at the enemy hill, I looked toward the city. I saw men walking about and children playing, and I could not go back. Toward evening my men began to abandon their positions one by one, slipping away to their homes. I tried to stop them. "Let them go," said my captain. "Soon they will come back anyway." I took my wife by the hand, and as we walked I told her about the hill. Every Saturday we go to look at it. Now and then I see my captain. Once, while sitting in the barber's chair to have my hair cut, I glanced in the mirror and saw my captain passing in the street. Sometimes my whole life passes before my eyes in the barber's mirror. I jumped from the chair. I paid for my haircut, and rushed out to the street to run after him. My captain was already gone.

Translated by Hillel Halkin

THE WORLD IS A ROOM

They returned by a different path from the one they had taken. They passed half a forest and came to a valley completely empty: Empty of stones and trees and people. From far away they heard the cries of children playing. He took out his camera and photographed her; then she photographed him. There's a snapshot of that wonderful day, in which the two of them are embracing. But how could that have happened? His camera wasn't automatic, and there was not a soul in the valley—a place empty as a star just discovered. Who then took the picture? Who watched their fate develop? Who held their weak smile opposite the light and saw it all?

They returned through Tivon, climbed a hill, her body went on divided: Her head was tired, all the childhood in her was tired, as was the sea in her eyes, tired with its anemones and longings. But her body strengthened with every step. He put his arm around her shoulders and her small head settled on it as if broken. He brought her back from the valley like someone returning her, dead.

They sat down in the small and only café in the place, where, at that moment, a wonderful tune was playing on the radio. Some long time later, it seemed to him that the war started just as the song ended, the last notes flowing into the first shots. Despite the fact that there were several hours between the two, in the distance of memory he heard the melody flowing into the first shots. That night everything in the country changed. The world's voice changed as at puberty; the world's voice became rough and husky, but the two never knew it, remembering only its pure voice.

They rose and paid for the coffee. They never forgot to pay—and they paid too for this tranquil evening with many nights of war. Lovers pay, never noticing prices, and they see no difference between the world empty of trees and people like their afternoon valley, and the world covered with other kinds of camouflage.

Afterward, they returned to the city. He entered his bachelor's room. The owners of the house weren't in, and he took a hot bath. When he finished, he rinsed the tub, watching the water go down the drain. It stirred his feelings about those last days of summer, going slowly, never to return.

At night, the resolution was passed to partition the country. People exploded into the streets, the firemen's band played, and the night of the bizarre dances began. She came to him like blessed amnesia. The din covered them as they sat together, and they hid beneath it. The great jubilation rolled like a huge ball through the night, bouncing around the heads of the celebrants. Where the

YEHUDA AMICHAI

—40—

two were not standing was a space through which the huge ball fell, rolling on till morning, becoming lost when the first shots were fired. Cars were already passing with pale, serious people looking out, hiding their ammunition; and other cars draped with first death.

After two days, or three, she saw a corpse for the first time. It was a woman. Shot to death, she lay on her side. It was then fashionable to emphasize the female contour. The dead woman also emphasized her womanly lines: her pelvis was raised and protruded as she lay on her side; her long hair was soaking in a sticky puddle of blood.

She volunteered to go down to the lower city, which was cut off from the rest of the city, surrounded by Arab houses. She served as a teacher in a small school, working with the children of Salonikan longshoremen from the harbor. One day the Arabs rolled barrels of explosives down the slope of the street. She and the children lay on the floor. When she got up she was covered with plaster and splinters of glass. That day she accompanied the children home. A British policeman guarded them. When they reached the main square, they were fired on from all sides, and there was no cover. The British policeman disappeared. She walked erect with her children, dividing the bullets like a sea. Snipers ran and repositioned themselves, but she crossed the empty square unbowed. Behind her the bullets closed again. A mantle always surrounds her: sometimes a heat wave, sometimes happiness . . . sometimes the war, as it did then. In the evenings the two of them would meet and their conversation became strange and fateful.

"I knew it," she said. "I knew that it would come this way."

"I think it's getting dark."

"Open the shutter."

"I opened it."

"Don't leave me."

"It's good to hear a full truck going down the hill."

"You're a good man."

"I think it's getting dark."

"It's as if they're sealing up the mouth of a cave on us."

"With stones."

"There are a lot of stones in the world."

"Once on Purim my mother had an attack of kidney stones: it's hard for me to imagine that inside my mother are stones like the stones on a mountain. It happened during a holiday dinner with guests at the table. My mother's pain wasn't theirs, only ours. So they left."

"I think it's already dark."

"Open the shutter."

Afterward he told her that in three days he would enlist in one of the combat units. He saw her home. They heard an explosion and the sound of bursting windows. She said to him that all the delicate objects in the world should be collected, everything fragile. Shop windows would perhaps be useful for coming generations, or for angels, who could set them in the window-frames of the firmament. People today are not used to caring for sensitive, fragile things: The first things broken in the world are those made of glass.

They passed the station of the Red Magen-David. A bullet-riddled bus pulled up full of wounded, its destination the first-aid station, not the bus terminal. They walked through the public garden. The path led between two flower-beds. A lantern here, a lantern there: The two came by, taking the light on their hair and on their shoulders. Later they sat and read about what had happened that day. They found a typographical error in the paper: Instead of saying "two of the fighters had fallen," they printed "two of the fiddlers had fallen." They thought it was a wonderful error—one of those mistakes that sharpen the meaning of the world and events. Like the mistake that began in her body, as she became heavy and wonderful, her head still narrow and girlish with sea-longing eyes.

On the third day he went away. He left her with his power-of-attorney—power-of-attorney over her own heart, now powerless. She was beautiful during their last night together, and his strength was beautiful with her. They felt happiness, which turned suddenly to an awful sadness. Among all the other things, she said to him: "We have a lot in common—a few books, season tickets to the symphony, a talent for getting used to any situation, a couple of other shared things." She wore a black skirt. Suddenly he said to her: "Those flowers in the pot know more about us than you would guess." He placed his desire in her keeping: "Here is what I will. I am going unwillingly." His watch was well-trained; otherwise it would have rebelled, missed the hour. Time is the etiquette of destiny.

When her bus started moving, he waved to her through the window grille. She rode home without finding a seat. She stood, her hands holding the straps. If her palms hadn't been busy holding her up in the swaying vehicle, she would have used them to wipe away her tears. So she stood, her thin face between her fingers, her armpits shouting like dark mouths, her mouth itself closed. At home she opened the refrigerator to eat something. She heard two or three explosions, then she heard a bitter cry. But it was a cry from her own throat.

He joined the division trying to break the siege of Jerusalem. Once he stood on the roof of a water-tower station next to the road. He had an hour of rest between engagements, and he wrote his name in black on the railing. Whenever his name is mentioned, people say, "Wait a minute, wait a minute, I know that name," not realizing that everyone who travels to Jerusalem has read his name many times. Now the wind and rains are blurring his name.

They started writing letters to each other. He was transferred to the south and again came to know different kinds of earth. He said to himself: "This war is like my lovemaking. I know many different kinds of earth. My forehead, or my chin or elbows or knees touch a rock or the sand or the fat earth. And thornbushes guard my tired head like sentinels." There were landscapes he knew only by night, as Isaac knew Jacob—a recognition by touch and the smell of the field. He didn't know whether to bless or curse. He was no hero, but he wasn't afraid.

After several battles fatigue overcame him. Once he fell asleep under fire. Destiny was also weary and made a mistake: They had sent a gunner to the unit; in error he was sent to the infantry. All over the country they were looking for gunners, and this fellow was sent to an infantry division. In one battle he was shot and he died. The fellow died by mistake. They retreated through terrible white sand, and the dead gunner lay stretched out on the railroad tracks now no longer in use.

In the group there had also been a British Christian named Shelley. All night, as they marched toward a battle that would end in retreat, he thought about the Englishman's name, like the name of the poet, whose works he certainly didn't know. The English volunteer used to wear a wide-brimmed tropical hat, in memory of the Empire in India. They met before the battle, when the group bivouacked among the ruins of an abandoned military camp. The buildings had blanched; you could see the kitchen that had been, the officers' club that had been, and the shower rooms. Later, in the first gunfire of morning, the Englishman Shelley died of the wounds he had sustained. His eyes died under the wide-brimmed tropical hat, and so died the memory of the poet with him.

What was left of the unit retreated to a kibbutz, in which there was no food because of the siege; so they ate matzahs. Then the kibbutz was shelled and everyone retreated by night through the half-devastated army camp. But before they left the kibbutz, he rested in a room whose occupants had evacuated. On the chest of drawers were a few ceramic objects, and on the shelf were books by Marx, a copy of Rosenzweig and Buber's translation of the Bible, and the poems of Rilke. Through the window were trees, and trees even farther off, near the enemy's emplacements.

The following day, airplanes passed overhead and everyone shouted, "They're ours! They're ours!" until a plane shot at them and began dropping bombs. When he got back to his foxhole near the hill, he wrote her a letter: "I'll be returning north in a little while. When the siege is over." Another time he wrote her: "When the clouds become rain, and the rain turns to fields, and the fields turn to joy, I will come." And he added that she shouldn't cry. She answered him by writing that the death of tears takes place in the desert, where everything ends.

The ancient wind blew from Mesopotamia and dried her tears and his sweat, and he no longer felt the hard days. Hard things die in softness: The stone sinks in the sand. Isaiah's hard words sink in the heart without effect. His hardened soul drowned in his love.

She also enlisted, and was sent to teach Hebrew to immigrant soldiers in the Galilee. One day he left the siege in an airplane for which they lit many torches on the dusty field; the next day he rode to Safed, where her unit was stationed. He crossed the bridge and reached the monastery, which served as headquarters. He went to the office: "Where are you from?" He explained where he had come from. He explained while looking out at Lake Tiberias through the window. For some time he had grown accustomed to gazing through windows; he thought it more important than looking at the man speaking to him. They sent him to the women's officer. There he was informed that his girlfriend had been injured in a car accident, and that she lay in a hospital in Haifa. The officer suggested that he spend the night, but he asked her if there was a ride to Haifa. There wasn't, and he went down to Rosh-Pina.

He waited for a car but none came by. It was getting dark. The world seemed to him an enormous room, the cities and villages in it, its furniture. He began walking toward Tiberias. The world was an enormous room, and at the far end of the room lay his girlfriend in bed. He walked in that direction, his steps echoing sharply. He heard voices behind him. And from the voices emerged two white blouses. The voices and blouses belonged to two young women from the neighboring kibbutz. Their pants were short and black like the night; only their bare legs and white blouses shone. Where was he from? He told them, and they discovered common acquaintances. The whole country was acquaintances, all of them in army divisions, in what's-his-name's regiment, some of them already dead.

They reached the kibbutz and he stood between the two voices, dumbfounded. They told him to come on in and stay the night. The kibbutz buildings rested on the slope of a high mountain, whose peak was invisible at night. He touched the hair of one girl and she said to him, "Come with us." He went with her to the kitchen, next to which was a trench with a cannon in it covered by netting. He ate with appetite in the big kitchen; only the two girls were around, serving him. Then a truck drove up whose driver they couldn't see because of the blackout, and they climbed in: At Ayelet-Hashahar there was a string quartet concert.

Gunners, other soldiers, and the members of the kibbutz were sitting in the dining room. He sat on a table with the two girls next to him, thinking: This is just like a fairy tale, just like a fairy tale.

They returned to the small kibbutz in the night; again no one was around but the two girls and a few camouflaged guns. They explained to him where the shower was and where the toilet. One of them came bringing freshly baked cake. Then he went with them to their room. It had a third bed. He removed his watch so that the band wouldn't press on his hand during the night. Then he took his papers out of his pocket, and put his Palmach insignia on the chair, the way armor was once removed. He lay down on his back fully dressed. They said to him, "There's hot water." He went out and they handed him a towel. He showered and heard through the jets of water the girls whispering to each other on the other side of the partition.

The night was fragrant with the smell of the buttercake that the girls had brought him, and the smell of the deserted lands. The two of them were still up reading. He excused himself for not chatting with them, because he was tired. They said to him, "You can take your clothes off. You don't have to be embarrassed. We're alone in the world with you and a couple of cannons covered with netting, like fish hauled up from the sea." He undressed and lay down naked. They also undressed; the three piles of clothes lay beside the three beds. Girls like them don't wear much in the summer, especially when they are alone during a cease-fire in fighting, beside the silent guns. The three of them lay down, each with eyes wide to the ceiling; they didn't go over to one another. He tried to time his breathing to the rhythm of their breathing, but couldn't. He didn't fall asleep, and lay wondering whether to go to them or not. They were good to him, they were young, and the world was an

THE WORLD IS A ROOM

—47—

empty room, in which only he was with them. Finally he saw that one of them had fallen asleep, and one was still awake. He went over to her; she made room for him to lie down by her side. He put the palm of his hand on the bones of her hip. She took his hand and put it on her flat stomach; her muscles quivered.

The next morning he woke up and saw that the girls' beds were already empty. He went down to the road, and caught a ride to Haifa. Once in Haifa he burst into the hospital, entered the ward and saw a long row of beds seemingly endless by perspective. When he was a boy he used to ask his father to sketch rooms and houses in perspective: to him it was a kind of magic. He had since learned to draw in perspective himself, and he well knew the measure of distance and the changes caused by distance.

She recovered and the war started up again. They saw each other during the cease-fires. Sometimes he felt the sharp mating-smell of his love for her. Suddenly he would feel her and not know how to deliver himself. Once he surprised her, and without her sensing him approach from behind, he put the palms of his hands over her eyes. "Guess who." And she, even though she knew who it was, didn't give the right answer. Similarly, fate would sometimes come to them and say "Guess who," and they would guess and guess: They guessed names of enemies and lovers and others, but they never guessed whose hand it really was. So the palms of the hands of fate remained on their eyes and they were blind.

Once she visited him in the army camp two days before the conquest of Beer-Sheva or some other place. They went out and saw a lone carob tree, and made love under it. He said to her, "See, we've done our part for settling the land. We've flattened the thistles, we've prepared the soil." That place was slightly higher than the surrounding southern region, and from it they radiated happiness on the lowlands. When they returned to camp, they entered the dining room, where the meal was already over. Sweet and sticky melon jelly, made in California, was gobbed on the tables among the hardening leftover bread. He pulled her toward him and kissed her. Others saw that she was his. There was whispering in the corners of the hall. The moon rose, and stood poised on a tank-gun standing in the yard.

The war didn't touch them at all. They were like ducks oiled against the water. She was busy with the problem of her heavy body and her childlike head; he with the problem of his future and the sight of landscapes through windows. Since they didn't struggle against fate or war, the war passed over them and didn't damage them. They were like an empty house with windows open, the wind passing right through them.

And this was their end: She married the soldier with whom she had overturned in the car, and with whom she had been injured. It was a neat and logical conclusion to a shared automobile accident, a shared tumble down an embankment in the mountains of the Upper Galilee. And he too, since he didn't fall in battle and was not wounded, is not of further interest to us. He was a man who didn't live in the shadow of his end. There are people who live in a valley beside a tall mountain that casts its shadow on them, influencing their lives and their ends. But he was not one of them. Nothing obligated him and nothing obligated her and the ties that once bound them were perhaps only illusory, as in stories.

Translated by Elinor Grumet

THE BAR MITZVAH PARTY

In the beginning was the rearrangement of furniture—in the big house, in the white stone house, across from the small café in which espresso steam rose day and night. The espresso machine was itself one of the many eternal lamps in the world. I came full of questions for my friends in the big house. They opened the door, and it was immediately clear that they had more questions than I did. We cancelled one another's questions out on balance, the remainder evaporating into the world like the cloud of coffee-fragrance across the street.

To reach them I had made my way through the gloomy stairwell. At first I couldn't find the button for the light. The button should have turned it on, but didn't. How can I complain? Even I only light up when switched on, and for some time there's been no button in me to summon up a large and happy light. I remain as gloomy as the stairwell, in which there is a sign downstairs, "No bicycle parking."

The whole family surrounded me, asking my help with the furniture rearrangement, to make room for all the guests coming the following day. We repositioned beds, and moved closets, and shoved tables. We blocked one sun, and made another spot sunny. The boy scooted among us, carrying light chairs and pillows, all the time humming a tune from his Haftorah. His voice was a bird's voice, and he himself was a young verse in the great Bible of the world. We were already clichéd verses, but he hadn't yet been memorized and moved in the world as in a great, white brain. We finished rearranging, and started over following new suggestions. Everything in the world begins with rearrangement: The night before one of the wars, I saw them moving men and convoys, vehicles and green and red crates, all night long. And they moved walls and they moved heavy earth. I knew there would be a war.

Another time I stood near the railway station on Friday evening. They were transferring various engines from track to track, from lane to lane, and I knew that I would change and would encounter unexpected things that might perhaps defeat me. At the very least, I knew that the wind would come, and that summer would end.

Once I had helped friends rearrange the furniture in their small apartment to make room for their new baby's crib. A few months later the baby died. A silence under the heaven of drying diapers. First the baby opened to life, then it closed up and died, like the drawer of a bureau pulled out and slammed shut that no locksmith can ever open again. After he died, we put the furniture back in place.

And when the seasons change, the world-stuff is rearranged: clouds, green earth, earth that's yellow and dry. People are perpetually being rearranged, nothing changing but externally, under the heaven of drying clouds.

I finished the moving, and rested near the window. I looked across at the espresso house; my wife was sitting there with one of her friends. The woman is several years her senior, and she wanders through her life, which is sizable—rattling around in it without filling it. At times she's like a door half shut, half open. All her actions are round-trip actions: She's like a person buying a round-trip ticket, but she never uses the second half. She never returns, even though that would be cheaper and more ethical. Her husband, who had been much older than me, died. Now that she is about to marry a senior officer in the Air Force, a lawyer she once loved has appeared on the scene. She calls him half affectionately, half in loathing "my misfortune," "my calamity," "my woe."

At any rate, there she was sitting next to my wife on a stool, her earrings large and round, her monkey-thoughts swinging in them. She was rolling her feelings into long, narrow cigarettes and smoking them one at a time. She was sitting and telling my wife about her love affairs, about her misfortune-sorrow-woe who bullies her, who doesn't leave her alone. Once he left her standing in the middle of the street when his taxi drove up. Another time he embraced her, looking way past her, over beyond an empty lot. Another time he asked her to write him poems describing his handsomeness and her love for him. She argued that she was no poet. He replied that if she really loved him she would rhapsodize for him in his praise.

She had already written him letters several times in which she said: "We're not going to see each other again. You've gone too far. You've strung the bow too tight and it's snapped. I don't love you anymore." She would write

and send off the letters, and the next day go back to him—
to her sorrow-calamity-woe-deeply beloved. The problem
is that she doesn't know how to say good-bye, so life isn't
any good. Most people know that their faces are farewell
faces. Just as the face of a clock is understood to be the
face of time, so the face of a human being is made expressly
for parting, and remembering or forgetting.

I sometimes know this, so my hands are always extended for a last handshake. They tell me, "You're crazy;
we'll see each other tomorrow." And I say, "This is the
last time."

The boy for whom all the furniture had been rearranged
came over to me, pulled me toward him, and asked me to
have a look at his presents. We wriggled through the amassed
furniture.

There were the knapsack and blanket for his future
outings. And a canteen and walking stick. Real exilic gear.
He said to me: "For hikes and the Youth Corps." I said to
myself: For separations; they're equipping him to accustom
himself slowly to wandering. Whoever starts wandering never
stops. The wind knows this and the clouds know and a few
people know—and not simply in autumn. There were a
knife, fork, and spoon folded together, and the rest of the
equipment folded up for the boy's coming sadness. A knife
and fork facilitate eating, but what helps us cut our fate-
portions politely? Maybe the yelling, the quiet weeping,
and the whispered words of brothers.

What other Bar Mitzvah gifts did the boy get? Multicolored pocket flashlights and thoughts entertained under
pressure. Binoculars that magnify and diminish, and other
instruments that adjust the look of things to our liking.
And black-banded t'fillin, and ways to bind the hand seven,
and again seven times. And fountain pens. And a book
about other people's heroic deeds. And Bialik and Tscher-

nikovsky and two pictures by Van Gogh, who cut off his ear. And encyclopedias that never get opened. And a toilet kit, and a kit for crying. And lots of blank paper. And lots of sheets of stationery with the boy's name printed at the top. And envelopes with his name printed on the back. If they could, they would have written out the letters themselves, the recipients' addresses, the love expressed in the letters, the requests and the anguish. And a briefcase for eventualities. A manicure kit in a red case. And handkerchiefs with his initials embroidered on them. And an empty and nameless destiny, and seven pocket knives, and a few records for dancing—a pastime sometimes helpful in evading death. And another manicure kit in a brown case for cleaning his nails, so that if he puts his hands over his eyes in despair, in order not to see what is going on, his nails will be clean and shiny. The palms of the hands go a long way before they come to be put on the eyes, at which point there is no other place to put them and there is no other place for the eyes to hide but in the hands: The beloved woman is not in the wall and not in the table and not in the neck. There was also a penknife in which openers and knives and small saws were folded together. And a small brain with several world-views. And the writings of Yosef Hayim Brenner. And a watch from his grandfather and an alarm clock from his aunt and many congratulations and expectations. And books of action and suspense, and books of moral instruction, and flashy sports pants with a red stripe. There was also a box of compasses on the gift table. All kinds of compasses shone on the black velvet of the box lining. The boy took out the instruments and showed me a shiny one. At this point he needs only a simple compass, and not the rest of them. Even if he becomes an engineer, he won't be able to use those instruments; he'll have to buy himself ones more precise. When, then, will he make use of this box? Most gifts are like that, and most of life passes that way—everything is either too late or too early. Once I was discharged from one of the armed forces in the summer. As I left the camp that was next to orchards, I saw that the oranges were small and green: I was too late and I was too early. I was too late for the trees' fragrant blossoming. I was too early for the ripe fruits, and I didn't know if I would be there in the autumn, when the oranges in the orchard would be ready.

There were no more gifts and no further need to re-arrange chairs. I took my leave of the family. The adults stood around me and thanked me with their hands. Their mouths were closed. Only the mouth of the boy was wide open, as if his upper lip were insufficiently large to shut it. His mouth stayed open in astonishment, and that open mouth of the boy is the world's way out: There is still hope. There is a place from which redemption will come, and through which it is possible to escape. The mouths of the adults were like the windows of a house bricked up into a wall. Here too, after many years, one could still see that there used to be a window in that wall that has since been bricked up. If the boy is bar-mitzvah'd, his open mouth will also be shut.

Then I went home. I don't know why my wife and I were invited to the celebration dinner. Maybe simply be-cause they knew us; maybe because we once stood under the same bird-fluttering sky; or maybe because some com-mon grandfather was discovered in one of the previous generations. On Friday evening we went to the resplendent club in Jerusalem in which the banquet was being held. They came and took us by car: We rode to the club in a black car. Near the steps were bushes, and in the bushes there was whispering about our hosts. Like, "Where did they get all the money?" They were always spending more money than they earned. The boy's parents were like that, and the grandfather and his wife, the grandmother. When I was a boy my parents would sometimes talk about such families who lived above their means. My father spoke about them with contempt, and my mother spoke fearing the calamity liable to befall them. I saw them, those care-free, wasteful families, and was terribly afraid that one day they would collapse. They were ringed with an atmosphere of mortgages, and loans, and IOUs past due, and pledges that never materialized, and dowries squandered on expen-sive fur coats. Outwardly everything was fine, unwrinkled, without tremors of worry, or memory of terrible yellow envelopes. We entered the hall above the wide staircase. Most of the staircases in our country are narrow. Jacob too dreamt about a narrow ladder and not the wide steps of churches.

The boy was waiting by the entrance. His head was awake and his mouth open. In a side room all the guests were already seated. We had barely entered when the sign was given and everyone ran to the table. Some of the relatives were hanging somewhere in heavy frames, and some within the frames of their lives, while others were between the two frameworks. So there remained empty areas, like windows with no one looking out from them.

The mother coaxed the guests to the table. Her body was thin and lithe and she looked younger than her age. She wore high-heeled shoes, shoes above her means. Her eyes slanted like the eyes of a Japanese and her smile, preserved from a period when she was happy in her life, was perpetual. She liked the smile and she left it like an invariant hairdo, like an ornament.

Twenty-five years earlier they had all immigrated to Palestine. The old people and their married sons came from northern Prussia and their speech was sharp and a little derisive. They came, and with them crates full of fur coats, carpets, many pieces of expensive china, and not a single hand tool. The old people were in business, and the boy's father, their son, was a lawyer. Several times already his heart had been stopped up by a plug formed in his blood, and he was always put back on his feet in order to live above his income. It wasn't comfortable for him to live at that elevation, like a pilot unused to heights. His lips trembled and he tried to keep his face tranquil, but was not successful. His wife, in the meantime, lingered among one and all, and conducted the guests to their seats, some with a touch of her fingertips, some with an elusive smile, and some by linking her arm through theirs. There was a bespectacled man there whose hair was long like an artist's. He had been a doctor, and was now a paper salesman and a devotee of religion and modern art. He sat on his chair and got up; a small nail protruded and the cloth tore. In that way he discovered that some door or other wasn't closed well and was making noise. There's nothing worse than a door or window that isn't well secured in its frame. The wind blows and the door knocks. And even when there isn't any wind, it moves. An alert black dog might just get in. It sets the curtains moving and you're never alone.

The bespectacled man sat down again and made the movement of a man closing a great cape across his chest— a regal, inflated gesture. When he was young his father had taught him a saying: "Look not at the vessel, but at what is in it." Since then he hasn't stopped looking into vessels. And he's always seeing something missing, a defect or a shortcoming. During the meal, he went out twice as if to examine seams that had ripped open in the family calm. They asked him why he had gone out and he answered with a shrug. The Old City was across the valley and it was dark, except for the clock tower that radiated its time.

When he returned he saw that there were cracks in the ceiling. He happened to hear two women in conversation who were so well hidden that they could have been sitting either behind the curtain or under the table. They spoke in a whisper. "She still looks young. How much did the dinner cost them? Where will they get the money from? And how skinny she is. And that smile. It isn't real. A smile above her means. And how lithe she is. She's not wearing anything."

The woman not wearing anything, the mother of the boy, was persuading the guests to eat. Her voice was skillful in its words. But her eyes were nervous. She was entirely preoccupied with covering her nakedness. Not the nakedness of her body, which was covered, but the nakedness in her whole environment, her life above her husband's earnings. Her speech, that was nervous, covered like the hands of a woman who is caught bathing nude and who covers her breasts. Her speech covered the cracks in her confidence.

Her husband, the lawyer, wore a black yarmulka. And those who didn't have yarmulkas covered their heads with a napkin or with the palms of their hands. The grandfather made kiddush with Ashkenazic syllables laced among Sephardic ones. He was old, tall, and thin. His head was the head of an old bird—a thin head, and on his forehead swelled a protuberance that alternately filled and emptied, like a strange signal of what was inside his brow. When he was young they said of him that he was a great wooer of beautiful women, and was even successful at it. "Apronchaser" they nicknamed him, "Don Juan." "A guy with fists behind his ears." All those epithets were in him. Except for the sign that stuck to him since and forevermore, that he was living beyond his means, for he was the Big-Daddy-of-all-who-live-beyond-their-means. In this way he reached eighty: He lived beyond his years. Lately he had begun to take stock of his soul and he saw that he must return a little to the bosom of religion. It's also possible that a disease of his urinary tract had brought him to these kinds of penitent meditations. Now he stood and said kiddush and held a candle in his trembling hand. The boy sudddenly burst out laughing, loud and ringingly. His mouth, which had in it the chance for a more beautiful world, was opened wide. His eyes were brown and clever and a lone lock of hair was dropped into the middle of his arched forehead. The eating got under way. The waiters, their noses sensitive to the difference between real and spurious wealth, felt immediately that there were cracks and fissures in the walls of conceit and in the ceiling of pretension. Immediately they became insolent, excessively and exaggeratedly servile, repeating often and emphasizing: "Yes, sir"; "Allow me, honorable madam"; "Yes, indeed, this fish is excellent— perhaps you would care for another piece"; "Absolutely, dear doctor sir"; "Of course"; "Always at your service," and other such words.

Grandpa rose and tapped his glass with his teaspoon, and everything quieted down. The protuberance on his forehead opened out and his black suit wound around him like a flag on a pole on a windless day. The fun-loving Paulina shot a fun-loving glance at all the drinking glasses and at all the eyes, some of which were full like glasses, and some already empty, after drinking. She was so fun-loving she had already married three or four husbands and had been divorced from them. And all the husbands were now dark and black and had disappeared from her life.

According to the laws of ballistics governing her fate, her joy in life was due to return to her. Or else she would reach the place of forgetfulness. In her memories, a specific color had been fixed to every one of her husbands, and to their names.

Old Grandpa had in the meantime begun making a speech. What did he talk about? About the good boy who is always a good boy. A nice topic, very edifying, but he didn't know how to finish his speech. Like a car with faulty brakes, the grandfather rolled down the slope of his speech, whose whole content concerned the good boy who will always be good. His wife, with the aristocratic face, pulled at his sleeve. "Jozef, Jozef, stop already!" But he didn't stop. Fun-loving Paulina looked at the boy, who sat next to his grandfather holding forth above him like a tower. Again the boy burst out laughing loudly. His father scolded him. Paulina's round hips quivered a little under her tight skirt and her small nose gleamed in enjoyment.

At last Grandpa sat down, folding his thin voice into his thin body like a penknife, and silence reigned. The waiters saved the situation by serving an additional course. They came among us like frisky dogs. They whispered a little something into the ears of some of the banqueters while serving. The bespectacled man rose from his seat; he closed his romantic imaginative jacket with a high-born wave of his arm and talked about the following day's Haftorah. Valiantly he tried to be equal to an evening of seriousness, but since everyone knew that along with religion he loved women and artist-types, his words were not esteemed. He sat down and put the palm of his hand on the knees of Aunt Lucy, who sat next to him. She allowed him to lay his hand. She's a widow, her husband having died only a year ago. It was rumored that she had been the mistress of one of the rich Christian Arabs in Talbiyeh. It was said that he had enormous dogs, St. Bernards, from whose mouths saliva constantly dripped in sheer ferocity. The gate of his house was black wrought-iron. She visited his apartment every day. He had a green sports car. Lucy's husband knew everything and didn't object. It was rumored that she used to ride one of the giant dogs naked right into the middle of the bedroom. The Arab also had a black, smartened-up car for evening with temperature control, a bar in the middle of the partition, and the entire back seat made over into a red divan. On which sat Aunt Lucy.

Then she had a British wing commander. There is no wing-commander so-called among angels and seraphs, only at the head of a wing of warplanes. Wings were embroidered on his jacket, and his eyes were bright as if viewing his life from its heights. There again her husband didn't interfere. She was a redhead and now she was around forty or fifty. Her husband died a year ago and the Arab now lives in Paris, having left his beautiful house to one of the consulates. What do consulates do? They dig around in the garbage to see what the population has been eating, and where its weakness lies, and where it is possible to uncover the vulnerability of the earth. Foreign flags are raised on the roofs of their houses, and on the lower floors they are always interrogating me and asking me different questions. The wing commander certainly fell and broke his wings and the ferocious dogs also died at the time of the war; there is no more sport in the sports car; and at night they speak a medley of tongues in the squares of Talbiyeh beside the gates of wrought-iron. Only the trees still know the differences and cut time with sharp branches. The boy saw that the art-lover had put the palm of his hand on Aunt Lucy's knees and laughed a third time.

There also sat a mother and daughter who resembled each other, and both of them had a big bared spot on their backs. At the end of the table sat another uncle silently. But inside him the speeches he was making to himself pulled at him. He was alone and a bachelor and had no wife to tug at his sleeve to get him to stop his speech. Instead of a wife, he had iron shrapnel in the flesh of his body. First you extract iron from mountains. Then you make bullets out of it that will enter the bodies of human beings. When human beings are buried and become dust, all that is left of them is the iron, which then returns to its mountains. There wasn't a great deal of iron in Uncle Max's body, but the iron sufficed him and lodged in his body, so he didn't take a wife. Since then thoughts stand in him like solitary men. Always in a mountain range, always solitary.

They continued to alternate speechmaking and eating. Whenever they ate, the fissures were invisible. It was when they made speeches that the cracks in the serenity were clear. All the faces became false. From time to time God nudged my knee under the table, signalling me to pay attention to a defect or shortcoming, signalling me to prophesy. And I actually saw the door that didn't close properly, and the varnish that was cracked on the piano. And I saw the insolence of the waiters bursting like a bright shirt through a jacket sleeve split at the elbow. I figured that pretty soon they would start spilling the food on us.

The meal ended and a photographer came and took pictures. Three times the flash failed to go off. Then everyone rose unwillingly from the tables and went into the other room, to the pictures of Trumpeldor and Weizmann and the other greats. The mother, who was wearing nothing, put one foot on the other and rocked back and forth in her black shoes. The round of dances started up. I danced with the fun-loving Paulina, her head covered with small, adorable curls. Her nose was small and on it sat a pair of glasses, because she was nearsighted. After separating from each husband, she became more beautiful and more fun-loving. Side doors were opened and dancers danced into the waiters' cloakroom. Hanging in there were white jackets and coats and swinging hangers without clothes on them. Paulina said that every time she's married she's like a hanger with clothes on it, and now that she's free she swings like the unencumbered hangers and she has it good.

We returned to the hall. The boy made a short speech. He said that he couldn't understand why everyone was so good. Tears came to people's eyes and the boy stopped when he saw what his little sentences were eliciting. The be-spectacled man took up the themes of religion and free love. "God . . ." he said, "God is like Mt. Everest: few succeed in understanding Him, though we all see Him from afar." Someone said, "And those who succeed in reaching the top take a picture and come down and write a big book." Then they started to take the guests home, except for two who stayed in the garden among the bushes, in a tree, whispering till dawn. Out in the world, doors were banging. I looked into Uncle Max's eyes and I saw the iron laid at his depths. I parted from the boy; his mother smiled as one smiles into a telephone receiver.

The following day we went to the synagogue. It was the house of prayer of German Jews; in it one stands erect and motionless before God. Everything was made of bright wood and there was no screen between the men and women. When a man looks for his mother or his lover among the worshippers, he finds her sitting next to him, in the wom-en's section perpendicular to the men's area, without a fence or lattice or curtain separating them.

This synagogue was built in a basement, and they put up a protective wall outside, with "Shelter" written on it. I was late in coming and I sat way in the back. An old man gave me a metal card with "sixth aliyah" written on it. I began to go over in my mind the blessings on going up to the Torah and those on leaving it and I confused the two. They opened the ark. It was lit up from inside like an electric refrigerator and the magic was dazzling. Then they started reading the Torah. Two old men sat on either side of me and handed one another pictures taken some time ago. Since I sat in the middle, I got to see all the pictures. I was a transfer-point, a kind of exchange market. Sometimes this sort of thing happens to me in thought, or with poems passing through me, that I transfer from side to side. Sometimes I am pressed between the two, sometimes in some way I disturb them. There were many snapshots, all taken in Germany. On one was a stone monument on which was carved a name in Hebrew characters; beside it grass, and still other rocks, and in the distance a mountain—half forest, half grass. In another picture sat four old men and women on a bench next to a huge chestnut tree, and next to the old people two Catholic nuns in their capacious costumes. Behind them was a house in the full bloom of dilapidation. Through its windows peeked sky and billowing linen.

They stood the Torah crown next to my bench. It was a small tower of bells made of silver. Since there are no bell-towers in synagogues as in churches, they have to make do with little belfries for the Torah scrolls. When they raised the Torah, afterward, the identity card of the man lifting it fell from his pocket. I picked it up and gave it to him once he was sitting, his hands embracing the scroll.

As I said, the synagogue was in a basement—with small windows at the edge of the ceiling. In the windows you could see legs from the knees down and nothing more. It was a good thing that I could see only the legs of the passersby and not their heads.

The portion that was read was from that closing book

in the Pentateuch in which Moses suddenly remembers many things. And like things remembered, his memories came up by association. Between the sections one can actually feel the smack-on-the-forehead and exclamations like, "Before I forget . . . Wait a minute, wait a minute! I'm not yet finished! What else did I want to say?!?" That is the source of the outpouring of ordinance: some speech coming fluently and some with difficulty, stutteringly, hesitantly, skipping from subject to subject. Not in vain was the forehead-banging, the effort of memory, and the exclamations. A hail of laws descended from them, among them difficult and strange ones, as given to the generation of the desert: parents stoning their son who won't obey them. War and ruin, and extermination of nations, and curses accompanying laws of nakedness. And don't sleep with your father's wives. And don't wear women's clothing. Terrible laws for terrible people. As, for example, the two disputants beating each other: two men raised by animals in the terrible desert. Then comes the wife of one to rescue her husband, and grabs the genitals of the stronger man. And they cut off her hand. All of those were read out in the sweet and melodious voice of the reader, who would again be a clerk in the Ministry of Justice the following day, and who never raised his hand against another man, and whose wife never needed to crush the genitals of his adversary. His sons, moreover, are well educated and say "hello" and "pardon me" and "please," and there is no need to stone them to death, and similarly no need for them to come to the basement synagogue.

The boy began to chant the Haftorah in a thin voice. It was the flageolet sound created on the violin by not pressing the string to the fingerboard, but using a hesitant touch that slightly tickles the finger. That was his voice. Voices that are fully developed are pressed well to the fingerboard; they are sometimes hard and sometimes sweet but always definite.

On a bench next to the reader's stand sat the boy's friends listening. Some were still children like him. And some were already growing up. There are several different ways in maturing: Some swell up a little as if they had been fried. Lips, cheeks, everything tightens and rises, and pretty soon the skin cracks. With a few, the skin doesn't know how to behave. It has no set agenda, there is no architect who knows how to build everything in just proportion. Then there are those who suddenly elongate. Life tugs at the head while their feet are still entangled in childhood. The body becomes long and thin to the outer limit of possibility. And the heart isn't yet able to supply blood to the entire elongated body—like a city that has suddenly spread out, in which the electric company has not yet had time to extend the network of poles and wires.

The boy's Haftorah wasn't long. He finished chanting it in a high voice, and his voice rose at the end as if in a question, the opposite of a rhetorical question: one with no answer. Suddenly I remembered—and when they closed the doors of the ark I knew for sure—there used to be an exercise hall in this very basement. The teacher, an old gal who'd never married, gave private exercise lessons to women with bellies, and heavy-moving teens, and weakling girls, so that they might master their own limbs. There were Swedish ladders against the walls, and mattresses and mats on the floor for exercising, and bicycle-riding in the air, and head-stands. In our country places transform themselves. The Arab village becomes an immigrant settlement. The garage becomes a school, and the mosque a cultural center. And so with people, who become transformed, only their faces staying the same. I who live in a nice house— my soul lives in tents lighter than the tents of the Bedouin.

I, who will sleep in my bed, will sleep outside, the hard stones pretending to be a soft mattress. In this basement Sarah once used to live.

The holy ark was closed and my memory was closed. They again closed the curtain on which was embroidered so-and-so's contribution in memory of his wife who had died in the bombing of Ben Yehudah Street, and the date was also embroidered. Everywhere there's a date embroidered. What is the source of the word "date"? "Given." What is given? Time is given. And time is long. Datelines are like lines on a thermometer. Time sickness is terrible.

Then the short, wide rabbi delivered his charge to the boy. The entire congregation was sitting, and he alone stood opposite the boy, leaning his elbow on the table, speaking to him on matters of tradition and religion and ethics. I saw my wife sitting in the women's section pretending to listen to his words, and I knew that she was listening to the words that I was saying inside myself, and not to those of the clean-shaven rabbi.

That same Herr Doktor Rabiner was a good and trustworthy man. He lived in the basement of another house, and so that anyone who needed spiritual support, or a wedding, or a eulogy, would find him, he set up a huge marble slab at the entrance to his house, with his name on it. What did the neighborhood kids do? One day they put a wreath of flowers on the huge marble slab, as on a grave.

In the afternoon all the children in the boy's class came and threw a party on the flat roof. They played question- and hollering- and singing-games. They also played a bottle game: Everyone sits in a circle. The one in the middle spins an empty bottle and asks a question. For example, who will marry first? The bottle spins until it comes to rest, its neck pointing to one of the people sitting. All of life is played according to the rules of a game. Whoever is ignorant must put up collateral: Sometimes they give a watch or a handkerchief. Sometimes they give a heart, or a hand, or a leg, or life itself.

In the evening they came and showed a film. They came and told me that Sarah wouldn't be back. I asked, What does that mean? Sarah wrote me that she was coming. But her little sister told me that she wasn't coming: She broke her spine and was staying put. And if she recovered she would return to her distant home. Sarah's little sister again mingled with the children and the film thrown from the black projector onto the white cloth passed beyond the roof's edge. There were live people in the film and they jumped and walked and talked on the cloth.

Suddenly I was alone. Alone like a telephone on a thin pole in an empty lot. That's how I felt at that moment, when I was told that Sarah wouldn't be back. The following day everything ended the way it had begun. It ended with the rearrangement of furniture. This time the articles of furniture were returned to their fixed places and the gifts were absorbed into the quotidian. And I knew that Sarah wouldn't return.

Translated by Elinor Grumet

TERRIBLE SPRING

In my hand I held a large paper bag with "Scrip to Israel" written on it.[*]

In that bag were Purim costumes that I wanted to return to their owner: a soldier's costume and a dancer's costume, the costumes of a ravaging pirate and of an earth-ravager, another sailor's suit, and the outfits of the angel of redemption and the angel of death. It was time to return those clothes. The characters were played out; the whispered prompting was quiet in the dark corners; and the nights had been returned to their cases, like musical in-

---

[*] *"Scrip to Israel" was the motto of a philanthropic system of food distribution in the early years of the state, when the Israeli economy was depressed.* —Trans.

struments after midnight. It would soon be Passover. Something always seems to be passing over: The angel of death passes over us and we name a holiday after him. Sometimes life passes over a man and he fails to live.

Those Purim costumes belonged to a woman whose husband was an actor on the Viennese stage in his time. When you visit, you sit with them in their small kitchen. The woman says to her husband: "And now do the part where you were the clown! And now do that thing where you laugh and cry at the same time."

He performs and we all have a good time; from their kitchen window you can see the Old City. Once he was an actor and now he is a clerk responsible for weights and measures. His wife, who owns the costumes, works in cosmetics. Once she was a nurse and healed the sick—now she makes them up. She makes Purim for them year-round with her paints and creams and facial masks. Sometimes she tires of her occupation. Sometimes she despairs at rearranging the face of affluence. And then she declares:

"You have to love. Not just in the spring. You have to take out your inner face. Everybody has an inner face and an outer face. When a person manages to take out his inner face, *then* he is beautiful. Like a soccer ball with an inner bladder—if you don't blow the bladder up, the ball won't be any good. Or like springtime, which brings out the inner face of the earth. Right, Walter? Now do Shylock in the courtroom."

That's what she says. They are good folk, and coffee is always brewing in their kitchen for people like me. Their stories and laughter and crying are also always brewing at their place as if on a low Sabbath flame. I came to them but they weren't at home. People aren't at home; sometimes they write on their door "Be Right Back," but they never come back.

YEHUDA AMICHAI

—72—

So I went over to my coffeehouse, the Little-Taste Café, opposite the Knesset building. It is small and narrow and drawn out like entrails. At one time the wall was made of small brown squares. Now it's painted a scaly yellow; a person could scratch himself on it, or tear back his skin like snakes do in the spring. Immediately on entering I saw two young people who had never frequented the Little-Taste before. Now they were sitting at the painters' table. It was early and the painters hadn't yet arrived, but when they would come the two would be forced to change their seats.

The painters come to the cafe every day and argue. Once an important minister died in Israel. The painters sat reclining, like the rabbis in the Haggadah on the night of Passover. A sculptor, one of their crowd, came in greatly excited and told them how he had been called at midnight to make the death mask of an illustrious deceased. They all got excited and envious. Some stranger was suddenly part of that hotly boisterous scene. So overstimulated were the painters that they spilled coffee on the stranger, smeared whipped cream on his face, and even tried to strangle him with the black telephone cord. Some of the painters are lonely. There is one who pays a stranger to call him up at the café. When called to the phone, he rises proudly and saunters over: "Yes. What? Please. When? I don't know if I can. I'm busy. My friend, I say I'm busy. We'll speak again, my friend."

A poet also makes his place there. He writes poems in Hungarian, and sits at the table adjoining the painters'. Instead of facing out into the street, he sits looking into the tiny kitchen of the Little-Taste. He has no idea what's happening outside the large front window. I once asked him how he could concentrate in all the tumult. He answered that he was like Titus in the legend, who had a gnat in his head that tormented him until he passed a black-smith's shop, when the gnat was quiet. The same thing happens to him: The din in the café silences the din in his head. Someday his inner cacophony will get used to that of the Little-Taste, and he'll have to find another noise—maybe at national assemblies or in factories—so that he'll be able to concentrate and write his poems.

Then I saw the two sitting. He in silence. She in silence. Suddenly I noticed that tears were running from her eyes. No, not tears running from her eyes, not tears, but small streams. Her big, open eyes filled like cups and streams flowed onto her cheeks. She wasn't sobbing; her crying was soundless. Her tears flowed unpreventable, like fate. He sat in silence, not looking at her, and she didn't look at him. Tears fell on the marble tabletop, and our good waitress Carmela wiped them up with a rag, just as she wipes up the stains of spilled coffee.

In came Mrs. Kunst, who makes the artistic carpets. Thin and bespectacled, she entered and said loudly in German, "*Kinder*, what are you sitting here for?! Go outside—it's spring!" And as she spoke, she fanned herself broadly with a bunch of cyclamen.

Nobody paid attention to her because the painters had not yet arrived. The Hungarian poet continued to look into the kitchen. He hates things that come in from outdoors. The young couple were busy—he with his silence, she with her unabating, streaming tears. Young people don't go outside in the spring. They sit in the corner of the Little-Taste in someone else's place and cry and practice silence. They try to understand one another. They would understand one another if only they went out into the season and picked cyclamen or wove artistic carpets. But spring hates lovers these days. It's terrible and frightening.

Mrs. Kunst sat herself down (since there was no other

place) next to the poet looking off into the refrigerator. When it opened she saw bright bottles, yellow containers, wonderful light—the whole world. Mrs. Kunst put the cyclamen on his sheets of paper. Flowers are good on blank white paper: a spring poem. She told him about springtime in the Jerusalem hills, but he was lazy, and even his poems were the fruit of his laziness.

Suddenly all the painters arrived. They routed the couple from their table—the painters and the sculptors and the carver of small wooden animals, who himself is a giant with a gray beard. The young woman asked Carmela for the key to the bathroom. You have to leave the café and cut across a courtyard in order to reach the bathroom, which is shared with the employees of a vegetable store. The young man waited. The painters began to argue over who and what was being shown at the Exhibition and at the Biennale and at other places. The mistress of the café watched the street with a critical eye, looking out at the world as she always did from behind the cake display in the big window. Members of the Knesset passed by. Children. A dog and a second dog. Another man. Another woman.

The young woman came back in. You could tell from her hair that it was windy outside, and from her tears that some terrible season was pressing in her blood. There was no need to go out; you just had to look at her. Mrs. Kunst would surely work her tears into a carpet. The painters grabbed their seats when the young couple left. Where was she from? What was the source of her unhappiness? Eventually Mintz, who makes woodcuts, came in. What's black on the wood comes out white in the print, and vice versa. Pretty Godlike work. In his house he has a collection of Japanese masks—some laughing, some pained, others terrified. There's a small Chinese bell on the door to his house that makes a pleasant sound when you enter. I love Mintz.

I went out into the terrible spring and entered the barbershop next door. When I'm anxious, I go to the barber's. He's also Godlike. He sits me in the chair, ties me up in a white cloth, and for all I know he could slit my throat. When he bends over me I can hear the ticking of his watch. I can see what's going on in the street in the mirror; I don't have to go outside or even turn my head. A young woman was sitting next to me. In this men's preserve? She wanted them to give her a man's haircut; she was an art student at Bezalel. Next to her leaned a big bag filled with blank pads of drawing paper. Her friend stood hesitating in the doorway. I saw it all in the mirror—her hesitation and abrupt entrance. She was entirely in black: black hair, black sweater, black skirt and socks. Where were the flowers? Where were the white dresses? Where was the green of spring? She flipped through some illustrated magazines. I was done and the barber shook my hairs from the sheet. The girl rose to take my place. "I won't let you cut your hair," I said to her.

"Why won't you let me?"

"Because it's spring."

"That means it's time for pruning."

I convinced her, and she agreed not to cut off her braids. The two friends left and I watched them disappear beside the well in which the great menorah is set. The barber started to sweep up my hairs, mixing them with others.

"What's in your carry-all?"

"It's just a paper bag."

"What's in your bag?"

"Masks and costumes. Everything I wanted to be."

"Lots of costumes."

I left and went a second time to the costumes' owner. In her hair there's a single almost playful white lock, and

I don't know whether her hair is really black and she bleaches just this one section, or if her hair is already white and she dyes it black, leaving this one white streak *zekher l'hurban*, "in memory of the destruction." A spring breeze whipped up paper in the street—the first stuff to flee in the general retreat. I stuck my free hand into my coat and tossed out all the scraps: ticket stubs of plays I'd seen, well-punched bus tickets. Sometimes you find a note from the year before. I let it all fly. There was a wrinkled black mask in my back pocket. I stuck my fingers in the eyeholes for eyes, then threw it away too. It landed in the street among the papers or in the lot or on the grass—a black mask on the bright lawn.

I went down King George Street. I saw a sign that said a hotel would soon be erected on the site. A hotel for meetings, or more surely for partings. It was decidedly a spring day. The first sun-shower started to gather behind the blue hills. I had already left many annotations on this street in my life, like marginal notes in a book. A passing girl said, "I'm covering myself with yellow flowers, because there are no violets." Next to a school two boys who had been kicked out of class were playing—free now, outside. I've been like that many times in my life, thrown out among yellow flowers by an infuriated teacher, short only of violets.

I saw a crowd gathering. A house was being demolished in an empty lot. They tear down the old houses when they are surrounded by new ones. The people stood at different distances, very silent as if looking in a mirror or watching a bullfight. They were silent and menacing. Then I saw the terrible sight: A single yellow bulldozer was storming the house, which was already half destroyed. It was a great clumsy house; one wanted to say that it was almost heavy-moving, like the last of an ancient race of elephants being annihilated by a young yellow tiger according to the rules of Darwin's game. It was a terrible battle—the confrontation of David and Goliath, with all the odds in favor of the small and cunning boy. David the yellow tiger.

My mother suddenly came to mind and tried to warn me. She always comes to warn me—about people, about drafts, about tigers, about houses being demolished. Meanwhile, in terrible silence, the people walked closer and closed up the spot where the terrible battle had just been engaged. Tourists whipped out cameras. Maybe they're demolishing the house for the tourists' sake, so they'll see what the young men of Israel are capable of, destroying and building. Their eyes will mist over: That young bulldozer driver, piloting his raging yellow chariot, is a hero! The closing crowd was silent, then someone yelled, "Don't get too close!" A boy with a black violin case in his hand stood among them. In his case was his reddish violin, which he had forgotten about. Somewhere his music teacher sat on her porch and waited for her lover, the spring breeze caressing her uncovered thighs. She forgot the boy. She asked herself, "Am I a witch? Maybe. I teach an innocent boy and desires are aroused." The innocent boy stood looking at the terrible springtime struggle.

The yellow bulldozer moved nimbly. First it tore down the walls of the house, pushing the ruins into mounds, so as to make a convenient approach to the other parts of the house. It gnawed at the corners of the foundation like a small animal sinking its teeth into the neck of one larger. The house cried out its pain and helplessness with great open windows.

It's not right. It's shameful. It's obscene. Again the bulldozer attacked. It tore open new wounds and enlarged old ones. It was like ripping a mouth open with bare hands. Like sticking fingernails in eye sockets. Without pausing, leaping and goring, the bulldozer descended on the brown, wounded house. My mother warned me a second time and disappeared. Everyone else remained. A monk stood next to me holding a prayer book. And then suddenly I saw the young woman who had been crying in the Little-Taste.

"You're not crying anymore."

"No, and I haven't been crying."

"But I saw you!"

"Spring cleaning. Will you look at this spectacle! I'm really turned on by this!" And in fact her eyes were sparkling like the eyes of women at the bullring in Barcelona.

"But it's terrible to watch this. There just isn't enough power to destroy an old house."

"It's wonderful! Like a dream of hitting your head against a wall. One that's collapsing."

"But it's a slaughter. It's unethical."

"Exactly."

"If you'd lived at the time of the Romans, you would have gotten a big kick out of the games at the Coliseum."

"No question."

"And just a minute ago you were crying in the cafe!"

"I wasn't crying."

With that, she turned from me and went toward the house. Growling violently, the bulldozer continued its assault. A single wall still stood in its place. The crowd held its breath in amazement as the wall fell beneath a single shove. The offices of the Missing Persons Location Center had been in the basement of that very building after the war. I once asked there after little Ruth who was incinerated. They knew nothing about her. My lover waited outside; I didn't want her to come in with me. In the office, they knew nothing about my lover, just as they knew nothing about little Ruth or the place of her ashes. Only I knew about her. Dust rose from the ruins. The tourists were happy! Israel was building! But I saw the house in its final agony. Showers of plaster and dirt flowed like blood from the windows, like small intestines spilling from wounds. Inner rooms were exposed, generations of shame and nakedness; inner walls in shocking colors—a pink, a green, a greenish, a baby blue—the colors of the underwear of a once-beautiful woman. Everything was exposed to the eye of the mob. The people were aroused, they were cruel in that terrible spring.

Next to the house stood a white tree blooming like the cloud of an explosion. A woman in black stood next to me. She was old.

"Look at the beautiful blossoms," I said.

"Not in front of the children! Watch your tongue!"

Across the way, a speedy waiter opened a coffeehouse, setting up folding chairs and tables, and putting down the tablecloths. The young woman who had been crying in the Little-Taste sat in a demolished room and dried the sweat from the brow of the driver of the bulldozer. She looked at the flowering tree through a hole torn in the rubble. The driver put the palm of his hand, black with oil, on her dress. She removed his hand and said, "Don't dirty the dress. You can dirty my skin. It's easier for me to wash than to have my dress cleaned." He rose, saying that it was time to finish the house. He lowered his goggles onto his eyes.

"I'll wait for you. And I'll watch you!"

"OK. But I'm not promising you anything."

"No matter."

"Afterward we'll smash a few walls of our own."

"I'll take care of myself."

He had small curls and looked like a Roman gladiator. He took off his shirt. His undershirt was black—as black as his hair, as black as the terrible spring. Springtime pushed up flowers and expanses of bright grass, but in its very center he was black and terrible, like blood.

YEHUDA AMICHAI

I waved goodbye to the woman. One arm was on the fellow's shoulder; with the other she waved goodbye to me. I knew her. When you approach most people, you stand and ring the bell. Behind the door you hear voices, scurrying, inner doors slamming. They are making their concealments, hiding, closing; only later will they open up to you. But in this girl there were no doors. Her face was open. There she was: crying in the café, laughing in the lot where a clumsy old building was being demolished. There she was in the terrible spring: dirtied with motor oil—her thighs, her whole body.

I picked up my bag of Purim costumes and walked toward Mamilah Park. They were redesigning it. Gardeners and engineers had been transferred, and now those who succeeded them were following a new plan, which would in turn be redrawn by their replacements. Once the Medrano Circus had been set up there. Now only the tentpoles remained. I passed through the Jewish cemetery. Spring covered everything.

It is a terrible urban process: People are buried outside the city; then the city expands and the cemeteries are suddenly among the houses. So again the dead are taken outside the city limits to a far hill. And again the city expands, and the new graves are also absorbed. And lovers too must go off some distance in order to make love and not be encompassed. But big cities in a hurry reach them too. Both lovers and the dead linger more now; they are slower.

My friends were still not home.

I went back to the lot; the bulldozer was still. Darkness was coming on. I stood next to a *Maskit* store, where they sell original clothes to tourists—garments that appear to be Yemenite or Russian or Arabic or from other countries. A foreigner came out of the store and asked me in his language if I could translate for him. He wanted a few dresses. What sizes? Assorted sizes. Afterward he asked me if I could spare a little time; he needed a translator. He was tall and alien. He ushered me into his car. It was the first warm evening—the smell of grass, and the smell of the first heat wave, the smell of dumped earth, and the smell of plaster from an old demolished house.

"Are you sure you have the time?"

In his language they often ask, "Are you sure?" No, I'm not sure. Even insurance companies couldn't guarantee my time this terrible spring. If there are flowers, can you be sure there will be fruit? He left me off at another friend's, one who lives in a shed in the middle of a garden. I went there because I was anxious and couldn't visit the barber at that hour. I noticed that a black car was standing near my friend's house. I hid behind a tree. My friend and the driver were taking an iron bed out of the house and putting it into the car. Why? What had happened? Then I recognized the tree I was standing under. Once, surprised by rain, we had stood under it; passing it the next day I saw how small it was and wondered how it had sheltered us the previous evening.

The next morning the foreigner appeared at my house while my wife and I were sitting having breakfast. He was agitated.

"Come quickly!"

"What's the matter?"

"I need you. You have to translate."

"I'm ready."

"Not the usual. It's a conversation with a woman."

"I'm ready."

He took me to the Little-Taste. I was proud when all the painters saw me alight from a magnificent automobile. The weeping young woman, who was again not crying, sat inside. The foreigner went over to her. She whispered to me, "You don't know me!"

The three of us went out and drove around.

"Ask her if she's free this evening."

"He wants to start up with you."

"Tell him I'm free this evening."

"She says she's free. What a run-around you are. You deserve a spanking."

"Undoubtedly. But I hate things that are good for me."

"Tell her that I want to stroll in the fields."

"He wants to get you in the grass."

"Tell him I'm amenable."

"And what about the driver of the bulldozer?"

"You're confusing me with somebody else. You were also wrong about my crying in the café, when I wasn't crying."

"What are you two chatting about? Just translate."

We walked out to a neighborhood of old Arab houses. In one yard stood a woman in a white apron who said, "In a little while there'll be a wedding here. I'm busy." Two young women, standing next to her, confirmed her words by nodding their heads—yes, there's to be a wedding. The foreigner said that during a spring like this the ceremony should be held after dark and the wedding night during the day, outdoors. I translated. We strolled in the fields. We chatted and I translated. We found some old shoes that had been discarded. You always find one lone shoe, always just one shoe thrown into the field. Where is the other one? I translated. Those people were fortunate who could slough off their skin like snakes in the springtime. I translated. The fields were all covered with people's skins. We talked and talked and I translated.

"I don't know what happens to me in the springtime."

"And in the summer you know?"

"In the summer I'm different."

"How's that?"

"Take the spring: When I'm by myself, I'm always wise and know what I'm doing. But when I come in contact with people, I get mixed up and disoriented."

"What are you talking about? Why aren't you translating? What is she saying?"

"That springtime is like her: disorganized. When she's at home she throws her clothes around. A dress here. A brassiere there. Underwear on the floor. A sock here and a sock there. Like the season that casts flowers randomly everywhere."

"Tell her that to me spring is terrible and black."

I translated.

"Tell her that at night I take off my watch and my ring. They disturb my sleep."

I translated.

The butcher came toward us, wearing his stained apron. He looked at the woman like a piece of meat for sale in his shop. I have always suspected that he keeps women in his big refrigerator; stairs connect the butcher shop with his apartment.

The foreigner bent over to fix something in his car. The young woman touched my jacket:

"You left a piece of paper inside."

"I threw everything away."

"You forgot a letter. You too. Get some sleep."

"Sleep doesn't solve everything."

"Even so: Sleep. Sleep."

"What is she saying?"

"She says she is going to sleep."

"No. She's coming with me to Athens."

"Is that so?"

The two left me. I told her to give regards to the owls in Athens. They drove off. I forgot to ask their names. But it wasn't important. Like in the movies, sometimes all the names of the actors appear at the beginning of the film, and sometimes at its conclusion. At the beginning I'm not yet interested, and at the end I still don't care to know the names.

I walked home to get the bag of Purim costumes. I knew that spring would pass and return terrible every year. I entered the house of the costumes' owners. The stairwell was always gloomy. The house was old. Suddenly in the black darkness a lunatic chirping of birds burst in on me. I didn't know where it came from. I ran up the stairs. I rang. They answered. I was saved.

Translated by Elinor Grumet

NINA
OF
ASHKELON

Once I had a summer girl who left me at summer's end. At first I thought when she left and autumn came that if she hadn't gone there would have been no autumn, that her leaving had caused the coming of autumn. Since then I have learned that there was no connection between the two events. There are many such parallel cycles: the cycle of seasons, the cycle of my life, the cycle of my loves, and that of my loneliness. Because of her and others too, and because of all of these, I was late going on my vacation to Ashkelon.

I came to the place like the Roman merchant who was buried there upon his return from a visit to southern Italy, his birthplace; he returned to the East and died. Artists were brought to decorate the interior of his grave. This same Roman merchant inspired various reflections and dreams in me. Not far from the hotel was his grave, in a hollow between two sand dunes.

People sitting on the grass in the hotel garden said: "One has to see the antiquities." Why are people in our country so excited about antiquities? Perhaps because the present is not certain, and the future less so. In ancient times they used to forecast the future. Now we program the past.

In the evening, the proprietor of the hotel strolled among his guests, delighted to see that they ate with gusto. He was red all over, like sausages boiled in water. Sometimes he put his hands on the table as if he wanted to serve himself up, so eager was he to please his guests. Aside from myself, the guests included a young couple who had been married the day before, and a muscular German woman with a strong, aggressive voice, and many others.

The next day we went to the historic excavations near the hotel. In the grave of the Roman merchant were some mosaics and broken pillars and marking places for the archaeologists—little notations like price tags in a shop window. Also there were chalk lines and wires strung about to aid the digging. We clustered around our guide. Once upon a time I hated to go to such places in an organized group. Now I loved the crowd, the closeness of bodies, the voices. Watch your step, behold, see the bas relief. Marvelous!

Sometimes I return alone to a place like this after having toured it with a group. And so it happened that in the evening I returned to the dead Roman's grave and sat in the soft, loose sand among the slips of paper and wires. On the road a car was passing slowly, like a police car, cruising, looking for something. Young men and women were sitting in the car, discussing whether they should stop and get out. Finally they drove on toward the tall tower in town. I studied the excavations. As in an architect's plan, you could see the foundations. This was house construction in reverse. The site had been turned into a plan, the plan flew into the builder's head, and from his head to the wide world.

I walked down to the sea and took off my shoes. The small crabs fled from me and disappeared into their holes, as did the sun, which was speeding toward the hole in the West where it would vanish. I watched the sun set while tying my sandals. We have learned to perform many actions simultaneously: I could sit tying on my sandals, sit and kneel and look toward the setting sun. If we are trained well, we can do three or four things together at the same time: ride in a car, cry, and look through a window; eat, love, think. And all the time consciousness passes like an elevator among the floors.

Later in the evening, a movie was shown in the garden. Everyone took a chair and sat down. Dogs and children ran about, draining off the attention of the audience; then they ran away and our attention returned to the preparations for the movie, the memory of supper, and gossip. The movie projectionists arrived late. A chair was placed on top of another chair to raise the projector to the proper height. The movie was about dancing, stabbing, and loving, all three of which seemed to be going on at the same time.

A girl passed between the screen and the projector. All the adventures mounted her back. I was jealous of her; she smiled. Her body moved in her dress as in a sea. Tomorrow she would go down once more to the soft beach. She did not have to labor much; life came her way, as readily as the movie that was now being shown on her white back. Two dogs jumped on each other. In a distant wing of the hotel a light went on. Someone left the audience. Someone didn't feel well. From the kitchen we heard the voice of a girl, singing.

The hotel owner said, "Later we shall go down to the beach and fry sausages." Those were his exact words. The movie ended and the chairs were left for the waiters to replace. We all descended to the beach. On the way we passed Shemuel's coffeehouse, where there were many pillars and a paved floor for dancing. That was Shemuel's coffeehouse. Shemuel had tried many things before he opened his coffeehouse near the sea that was black by night and green by day. That evening he had strung colored bulbs in happy chains in the sky of his coffeehouse, along the tops of the pillars which surrounded the dance floor. He governed his skies with the help of electric wires at night, and by day with canvas awnings that fenced out the noonday sun. That evening, soldiers from a nearby camp sat under his skies near the whispery sand. They had come to celebrate a victory, or to be comforted after defeat. At any rate, they had come to rest from the training grounds, the outposts, and the army offices. Silken girls put fumbling hands on their shoulders. Girls with rosy ice-cream thighs and eyes of chocolate cake. Whispering sand-girls who kept their warmth at night. Some of the soldiers had come with their heavy boots on, and danced like bears, swayed like drunkards. Shemuel looked upon all of them with pleasure and satisfaction; every once in a while he took a tray and passed among the dancers to attend to their wishes. We decided to postpone the sausage business until the following night. Some of the older women wanted to stay and watch the young soldiers dance. We sat with the local doctor. He nudged my shoulder and said: "Look, there is Shemuel's beautiful wife."

YEHUDA AMICHAI
—90—

She was standing near the exit, in front of a sign which said: "Discount for soldiers. Today—shashlik and liver." She had green eyes and a week ago she had returned to her husband. Once, a rich American had come to Ashkelon and she had run after him—literally. They had exchanged a few words while she served him in her husband's restaurant, then, simple as it sounds, she ran to the kitchen, threw off her apron, and ran after him across the sands through the thin bushes. That is to say, sitting in his hotel room in the town of Ashkelon, he did not yet know that she was pursuing him. Her shoes had filled with sand and she threw them away; she almost did the same with her skirt and lace panties. All these things—shoes, clothes, strange thoughts, the outgrowths of culture—disturbed her in her flight and her green eyes were those of a wildcat in an ancient forest. It was early morning when she arrived at the American's room. The next day she married him and they left together. After three months she returned. It is not to be supposed that she crossed the sea on her own power, although she was an able swimmer and fully capable of leaving her clothes in a heap near the shore in Naples and swimming to the shores of Israel. How and why they parted was not known.

Anyway, she came back through the sands, without a suitcase and clad in the same dress she had been wearing when she left; she was tired and barefoot. A week ago the exact same thing happened; she came back, disheveled, from a similar adventure, and refused to utter a word. She had to be taught to speak all over again.

That evening, as I have said, she stood near the exit, framed by the large sign, green-eyed, nose in the air, her mouth large and quiet in her white traveler's face. The fat doctor looked her over and said: "She is ready for new sands and new dances. That one will never be cured. She's like a Siamese twin to the whole world. A new American will come, or even a Greek or a Roman, as they used to come here in ancient days, and she will run after him." The doctor pointed to the Roman's tomb and fell silent.

One of the officers on the dance floor went out, picked some narcissus flowers, and handed them to her. She said to him: "I know their scent." He answered: "I do not yet know yours." She said: "For you it is not worthwhile." Her husband was not jealous, and he permitted the officer to hand her the flowers. Shemuel had learned not to be jealous. Every day he wrote out the menu on the board in front of which his wife was now standing. He knew what was to be served at the noon meal, and he knew whether there would be a dance for the soldiers in the evening. But he didn't know if his wife would stay with him.

A dog ran after a moth but failed to trap it. A soldier caught his girl while dancing and lifted her up, swung her about like a young palm branch so that she would bring him a blessing. Shemuel's wife stood still, as if she were examining cloth in a shop. Her eyes were open. The moth tried to fly into her eyes; she shut her lids. The elderly guests returned to the hotel. The doctor stayed with us. The soldiers returned to camp. No one blew the bugle.

At breakfast, conversation was lively. Plans for the day were spread out on the tables. Most of the women came down in shorts; the older the woman, the shorter the shorts. After the meal I strolled out toward the bushes, to the site of ancient Ashkelon. I had seen the area by night, surrounded and protected from the three winds by a rampart on which could be seen the remains of walls and towers, and in the west the sea. At night it had looked foreboding and somber, like a snarled entanglement with no exit. So I had decided to explore the area by morning light.

Still, the moment I entered the tangled bushes, my mood became blunt and heavy; I felt threatened. After walking a few hundred yards down the blue road, I reached the edge of the ancient town site. My feet sank into the flourlike sand. Instantly I found myself in a deserted orange grove. In our country we are used to deserted places, to seeing houses without roofs, windows without houses, bodies without life, blackened plantations, and the remains of cracked roads. But nothing ever nauseated me as much as that orange grove. The dead branches were covered with white snails; the whole grove seemed stricken with leprosy. I stared at the broken aqueducts, partly filled by sand from the sea. Thorns at once beautiful and terrible twined their way to the tops of the branches. There were dark corners among the trees that were too large, too large for their own good: ruined corners that guarded the sterility of their shadows. Green flies buzzed around the sweat on my forehead. I continued walking. Fat fruits dropped from sycamore trees and burst on the ground. Everywhere there was the depressing sensation of sand over dead bodies, of dead bodies over the earth. Sand flies burst in a cloud. The road turned, pathways opened, leading into thickets of tamarisks, pathways at the end of which anything at all might happen. A lair of dark curses in various Mediterranean tongues, the vomit of cultures torn from their homelands and transported here. Now this unholy thicket had all those layers beneath it. Such Mediterranean trickery! Phoenician merchants, Greek merchants, Jewish merchants—striking bargains with heaven and with the dead, bringing the smell of perfume and expensive cloth to the detriment of the native population. It is like this: a skeleton, but not yet a clean skeleton;

the odor of a rotting cadaver. I do not mean the odor of the coyotes and wildcats that die night after night in this thicket among the salted branches covered with snails. Such an odor would not nauseate me as did the sweet smell of this skeleton, but not yet a skeleton, of the ancient cultures rotting here in this thicket.

Here, for example, is a sycamore tree, leaning sideways in an unnatural fashion. I know there are trees near the sea and on the slopes that have been bent by the wind, but these sycamores had been permanently twisted by some intrinsic, predetermined corruptness. This landscape had been prostituted, pampered, spoiled. It destroyed its stomach on sweets. It should not pretend now to have a face of white marble, a girl's face, the tanned face of a soldier. All that is conjuring.

But I, at least, knew what lay underneath, what nourished the sycamores and the groves, what had really caused the marble pillars to be built. Even those narcissus flowers, so innocent in their whiteness—where did they get that exaggerated scent? It did not come from the sand. Indeed, it is best not to inquire what is in their roots. And those flies of Beelzebub that prey on live bodies and sculptures alike? I speak here of things which have refused to die, that continue an underground existence, beneath the sand and beneath the water, like submerged and incoherent whispers. A landscape that tosses in its bed with wild dreams. And what about that figure of Pan in the Roman's grave? By what metamorphosis did it arrive on this shore? And Shemuel's wife—where was she from? How did she escape, running through the sands, through the sea? And her green eyes?

I went on until I reached the small amphitheater where statues and broken mosaic tiles and Greek ledges lay about in disorder. Every historical period had collected in this hole, as in a textbook. The wind rose from the sea and the trees leaned toward the east.

From the amphitheater I took a side trail and walked down past one of the terrible sycamores that bent almost to the earth—that is to say, it was still standing, but in repose. The sycamore was not dead, because the ends of its branches sprouted leaves and sickening fat fruits. An old, crumbling wellhouse stood there, with an apparatus made of a double chain and small rectangular scoops for drawing water. I did what every man does when he passes a well: I threw a stone into it, but I heard nothing, neither the sound of water nor the smack of stone on stone. I threw a second stone, but nothing happened. I tried to pull the draw chain. I bent over and suddenly I felt myself covered with a cold sweat. I turned around.

Shemuel's wife was sitting on the trunk of the sycamore, swinging. She bared her teeth:

"Such a one as you are then, a snooper."

"Where do you know me from?"

"You—don't you live in the hotel?"

"Yes . . . but you . . ."

"Yesterday you were sitting with the fat doctor. He is also my doctor. How funny he is. When he examined me after I came back he wanted to kiss me. He's the same size as the Roman merchant buried in the sands."

"What do you know about the merchant?"

"And what are you looking for underneath this town?"

"I'm not looking for anything."

All that time she was sitting swinging on that evil tree. Then she asked me:

"Have you been to the ancient harbor already?"

Again she bared her teeth, then jumped off the tree in a bound and disappeared down one of the trails, parting the bushes with her hands to work her way through. The bushes sprang back after she passed. I was still standing near the old well. Nothing had changed here, I saw. This landscape was no more strange and terrible today than it was a week ago, years ago, millennia ago. Shemuel's wife could as easily have sat in the private amphitheater watching two wrestlers as she stood last night on the dance floor, watching the soldiers. I can imagine one of the wrestlers felling his opponent, then kneeling over him, gripping him with tong-like thighs while looking up at her for further instructions. She sticks to character: "Continue to the death!" The results are known. One of the two, the one lying upon the ground, grapples the other's chest with such force that a jet of blood breaks from his nostrils. The results are well known, known to this landscape, to the sycamore, to the marble, and to the wife of Shemuel, who pretends.

I went to the harbor and stood on the hill where the pillars faced the sea and there were no ships. In the distance I saw the beach. A whitened skeleton of a cat lay in the deep grass. Near it were a yellow paper and empty cans. I saw that I was standing above some Arab houses. Suddenly I heard a voice calling me; it was the masculine woman from the hotel. All this time I had tried to avoid her, but now I was happy to see her waving to me from the trail. At once the spell vanished. Together we climbed the sand ramparts above which stood the remnants of an ancient wall. She said: "I saw Shemuel's wife, the one from last night. She's a whore. Do you like her?" As she said this she poked me in the chest with her fist and laughed in a coarse, masculine manner. "When I was young, the men looked for sporty girls. I was good at winter sports. I caught my husband on a steep slope in the Alps. What do young men look for today? Fluttering, spoiled, green-eyed elastic-limbed females like Shemuel's wife."

In the midst of this one-sided conversation we reached the orange groves at the entrance to the ancient town. I discovered that many of the trees bore green fruit. It was the end of summer and yet the fruit had not ripened. On a single, broken branch, two oranges were yellowing in sterile, premature ripeness.

Before arriving at the hotel I took leave of my sportive companion, and was again rewarded with a punch that shook me to my bones. I went down to the sea. This time the beach was empty. I had not realized that I had spent almost a whole day on the site of ancient Ashkelon. A blackbird perched on a pillar that had once been consecrated to the gods. Two girls rolled in the sand and shouted. The sea left lines in the sand, but it was impossible to read the future in the palm of this shore. I ran after a crab that was sparkling with a strange silver color, but the silver—a tiny fish, the crab's prey—disappeared. The tamarisks finished their preparations for the night. The sun began to descend into the sea. When I returned to the hotel I was once more surprised by the amount of time that had passed.

After supper, the red-faced hotel keeper donned a white hat and apron. With a huge fork in his hand, he entered the reading room: "Be ready to go down to the sea." Two cooks were kept busy transporting a large stove to the beach; one of the young hotel maids adorned her neck with chains of red sausages, the way daughters of the Hawaiian Islands decorate themselves with flower chains. A merry procession then made its way to the sands. The young married couple preferred not to join us, but remained seated in the reading room. They had not yet acquired an apartment, and they wanted to make believe they owned the hotel.

The landlord and masculine woman did most of the talking. It did their hearts good to be on the beach, so they began singing, first a Hebrew song, then German hiking songs. The landlord's white hat served to illuminate the way for us. The sea was lazy that night and the moon had not yet come up. The cooks placed the stove on the sand and began stoking it with charcoal. Everyone was enchanted with the blaze, especially those who were close to the stove. Behind us dozed the somber mass of ancient Ashkelon. I did not sit close to the fire. We finished eating the sausages. Then came watermelon, and after the watermelon there were party games. One or two people would leave the group; the rest sat around in a circle, whispering. Then the people who left were called back; they were supposed to guess the plans of those who were sitting in the circle. Later, someone brought out a drum and a harmonica and everyone became sad. Still later they started dancing.

"Let's dance barefoot!" The hotel owner began to worry about the good name of his hotel, and about the welfare of the stove. He told the cooks to take the stove back to the hotel. Some people came from Shemuel's café—a few officers, some girl soldiers, the doctor and his quiet wife, and also Shemuel and his wife. At first they participated in the dancing and singing, then they split into separate groups. Suddenly, Shemuel's wife got up and ran in the direction of the waves. She left her shoes near me. The doctor said: "It is nothing. That is always her custom. It is a sort of courtesy visit she pays to the sea."

After a few minutes she came back, all wild and untidy and strange, the hems of her dress wet like lips after drinking. She caught up the hem of her dress and squeezed water out of it and bared her teeth in my face like a terrible biting animal. I saw that her watch had gotten wet. She took off her watch and held it between her teeth.

I told her: "Your watch got wet."

She took her watch out of her mouth and put it next

to my ear. Then she walked away. From walking she switched to jumping and from jumping to high, wonderful dance steps near the sea. When she returned, she said to me, "This is a *mitzvah* dance."

I said: "What's possessed you, Penina?"

She laughed and said: "My name is not Penina. They call me Nina."

"A nice name that is."

"That isn't the entire name. They call me Nina the Seagull."

Her voice was hoarse, as if lined with salt and seaweed. Shemuel approached and said:

"Here is a crate brought here by the sea. Once the sea brought a crate full of sardines. Once it brought a young dead whale. The sea brings many strange things. It brings things to my wife too. Sometimes in the morning I see strange objects lying near her sleeping body, like branches, like snails, like objects from an ancient ship that foundered on the rocks. Maybe you could tell me what to do about her?"

"Get her pregnant."

Shemuel laughed, and sighed, and then became silent. Later, one of the officers suggested playing tag near the sea. I remained sitting with Shemuel, who was slow. The doctor took part in the game, then he joined us. Because of his fat belly he couldn't keep running very long. Shemuel stopped talking when the doctor approached. Suddenly we heard screams and laughter and before I knew what had happened Nina jumped up and hid behind me. A young officer passed by us, running in great strides; he didn't realize that she was hiding. Nina's heart was beating hard.

The moon began to rise. Everybody put on bathing suits and went into the sea. Nina's voice was hoarse. All that she left behind in the world was her little bundle of clothes on the wide sands. The doctor said: "After all, God Himself is like that. He is far away from us, and all He left behind is a little pack of clothes on the vast sand, and to us that seems like God." Nina screamed from the sea. I rose in alarm, but the doctor calmed me: "That is her custom. Don't be alarmed." I left the doctor and Shemuel and God and Nina's parcel of clothes and joined another group. The masculine woman was among them, demonstrating such heroic feats as running fast, lifting rocks, and other manly deeds. The soldiers stood around her. Some tried to race with her, but she always won. When I approached she shouted: "Come, come!"

Afterward they brought drinks and we drank and the night never became cold. They made a fire in the sand out of old crates. I heard a whisper, a moan: "Get me out! Get me out!" Nobody heard it but me. I went in the direction of the voice. Nina was buried up to her hips in the sand, like a statue found on the beach, laughing. I uncovered her.

"Why don't you ask me? Sometimes intelligent people and artists come from the city and they are glad to find an interesting type like me."

"If I asked, you would lie to me anyway."

"But that, too, is a truth."

"I was convinced you had a fish tail like the daughters of the sea."

"Come with me to the hotel bar," Nina said.

I agreed; we went up to the hotel in our bathing suits. In came the suntanned Roman merchant and sat with us at the bar. There was no bartender because the hour was late. I went behind the bar and served them. The Roman looked in my direction and said: "Who is he?"

Nina said: "He's mine. I caught him in the sea."

The merchant looked at me from under his short, curly hair and said: "He is good for the big games in the arena." They both laughed until I fell asleep.

I woke up as the first morning chill penetrated the room. I heard a car stop; a man jumped out and called for the café owner. I came out wearing pajamas. The man seemed to have come from afar; he asked me: "Are you the café owner?" I explained that I was not the café owner and that this was a hotel. I could not see clearly in the early dawn.

He said: "Never mind. Come quick!"

I climbed into his car and we drove the length of the shore road in the direction of the dunes. He stopped the car in the high grass, jumped out and ran toward the sea. A woman was lying under a rough army blanket. I was alarmed.

"Don't be afraid," my companion said. Angrily, he pulled the blanket from the figure. The woman was nude. She woke up instantly. It was Nina.

"What are you doing here?" I asked.

"Are you a worrier too? Enough people worry about me."

I told her: "Come back with me to your home."

She laughed: "I have no clothes. He took my clothes as a pawn."

I advised her to cover herself with the blanket. The man who drove me out said: "The blanket is mine. I was passing by and saw a woman lying nude on the sand by the first light of dawn, and I covered her." Finally he agreed to drive us home. On the way she cried on my shoulder.

Shemuel was waiting at the gate of his house. All that day Nina didn't show up at the beach. I sat in the sand by myself and felt the first winds of autumn. Many of the awnings that had been spread against the summer sun were now torn. Papers were flying about or lay on the beach, covered with sand. A group of soldiers, boys and girls, arranged themselves to be photographed, then rearranged themselves after each snapshot. The ones who were standing lay down, a boy put his hand on a girl's shoulder, they posed in profile, then in groups of two and five, and then they all lay down as if dead. The two girls I had seen earlier rolling in the sand came over. They were still laughing and rolling. One of them wore a red bathing suit and her face was loud with pleasure. Everyone cleared a passage for them and they rolled on by us. The place where we had sat the night before was already covered with new sand. The old people sat in red lounge chairs and looked at the sea and waited in silence for death—hoping that death, too, would come to them in silence. Where do they derive their certainty that death will come from the west?

Near the lifeguard's tower a crowd had gathered. Two women undressed underneath a towel, twisting like snakes so as not to reveal their bodies. The lifeguard's skin was covered with tattoos and drawings of daughters of the sea, flowers, and an anchor in deep grass. People dragged up lounge chairs. A woman came out dressed in a white apron embroidered with the Star of David. She turned to me: "Do you see that blanket? The gray one?"

"Yes, I see it."

"Yesterday it was used to cover a dead man who had drowned."

A girl walked by, arm-in-arm with a young man. The camera hanging on his bare chest was like a third eye. They chatted together, then the girl began to leap in happy dancing steps. She ran up to a sandstone boulder, leaned against it with her hands folded behind her back, her face to the sea. There she stood like Andromeda in the Greek legend, waiting for her savior. She wore a helpless smile. The lifeguard, big and husky, walked toward her with a camera in his hands. She stood against the rock; there was no place for her to hide. He came closer, raised a hand as if to hold up a sword, counted aloud, one, two, three, and the girl, saved, jumped against him. But he was too busy turning knobs, keeping the pictures in order.

Later, the afternoon games began. Mothers called their children. All the gods in heaven and on earth called their prophets, who began to prophesy without pity, near the terrible woods and the sea. Toward nightfall everything awoke, and the foreign sea gurgled in small waves toward the beach. People shook the sand from their bodies as if preparing for the resurrection. Some of them walked over to the concrete breakwater, where they sat emptying the sand from their sandals and stockings and hair. They were all in a hurry to forget the sea. The shoreline, too, was in a hurry, and raced to join the sea and the sandstone wall at the horizon. I knew it was a false joining, a play of perspective. Everything was an illusion of the eyes. The children's cries, too, joined the great silence on the horizon. And everything covered itself with the somber soft grass of night. The sea's thoughts were dry and empty like darkening ears of corn thrown onto the sand. Everything was burnt.

I lay for a short while longer in the sand, watching the feet of those returning home. Then I too returned to the hotel, where I saw Nina sitting on the terrace. Her limbs were elastic and brown from a surfeit of sun. She was wearing red shorts that were so tight I could see the crease of her buttocks. I sat next to her, behind a bush that had provided a screen for us. She rested her feet on the railing, lifting her legs until they looked like a gate, like wings.

Then she laughed: "This morning you were quite alarmed—this morning when he awakened you and you found me lying among the weeds at dawn."

We watched a procession of black ants traverse the terrace floor. Nina put on her glasses and took a letter out of her purse. I asked if it was from an admirer. She said she had no admirer because one did not admire her but became crazy about her. Did it please her to have men become crazed at the sight of her face? Why not? Why, then, did she, too, become crazed when she lay out on the sands covered by a strange blanket? She was infected by the craziness of the crazed. There was nothing left for me to say to her. Nina took out her hairpins, letting her hair fall. Her hair flowed down to her waist, to her hips. And my thoughts at that instant were unknit and wild.

In the evening I took leave from Shemuel, her good husband. The next day I was to return to my town. Shemuel received me by himself. We talked about all the subjects in the world but Nina. Each time we felt the conversation coming around to Nina I led him around the subject without fail. Later, I got up to say goodbye. The bedroom door was open and I saw Nina lying in bed. One of her eyes was hidden by the pillow. The second was awake and open. For me, it will never close.

The next day I returned home and right away started work and forgot everything. My profession is to forget; it is my fate to remember. One evening I forgot to shut off the radio after the news broadcast. I went to shut it off when they began to announce that the Israeli police were asking for the public's help to locate a certain Nina. They mentioned her family name. Last seen wearing a striped white skirt and a white blouse with rolled-up sleeves. I returned to my guests and remained silent. How had I seen her last? Dressed in short red pants and with her hair loose. We sat up until midnight and talked about the announcements that are made to the public concerning missing persons. One of my guests said that it was all exaggerated. No sooner does someone go to visit his friends than everybody gets alarmed and announces on the radio that he is lost. Many people get lost in the world. Some of them are announced, some not. I told my guests that in Nina's case it was very serious and that I knew her. At midnight I suddenly heard voices coming from one of the houses nearby. A woman was screaming through her tears: "Go away! Leave me alone, you bastard!" I stood near the window. I saw nothing and then the voices stopped. A train whistled as it passed through the valley. It seemed to me that I had heard Nina's voice. Maybe she needed help. Maybe she was hiding in one of the houses in the neighborhood. The suntanned Roman, who once sat with us at the bar, must have kidnapped her. Maybe they were still hiding around Ashkelon, in the white sands, among the statues.

The following day there was another call for help on the radio. But in this broadcast Nina was described as wearing red pants and with her hair wild. They also announced the languages she knew, and some of the special habits she had, like pulling up her knees, and such personal characteristics as the smile in her eyes. I remembered her with one eye hidden in the pillow and one eye awake and staring. Poor Nina—she must certainly be very tired, wandering through the world with a Roman who wore the uniform of a UN officer. I was sure that he would treat her rudely whenever she became tired or asked for a few minutes' rest by the side of the blue road.

And so the two of them wandered about, hiding from time to time in various places. Once they hid at the house of her girlfriend, who was an expert manicurist. In the same building there was a movie theater, and her friend's apartment adjoined the projection booth and loudspeakers. The sound track could be heard on the staircase. I came in haste but Nina was not there. Her friend asked me if I wanted a manicure.

Then they hid in the Caves of the Judges in Sanhedria. Nina sat, her head leaning on his chest; she was pulling and tearing at the hair on his bare chest. Near them was a radio in a small suitcase. To the police description of Nina the Roman added his own: her breasts are brown and small, her thighs are fast and never rest.

On the next news bulletin they again detailed the languages Nina knew. All the Mediterranean tongues: a little bit of Greek and a little Italian and Spanish and Hebrew and a bit of Arabic.

One night, walking along the street, I saw a display window that was still lit. It belonged to a dress shop. One of the big mannequins in the window moved and I saw that it was Nina. Quickly she came out to me and said, "Be quiet, be quiet, don't say a thing." Also, she said that it had become impossible for her to imagine his hands without his voice, nor his eyes without his blood, and at last she said: "I am happy in my wanderings. Don't reveal anything to anyone, otherwise I will die."

I told her: "All this will end in a terrible fall, like the fall of the sycamore fruits."

They began to change their clothing from time to time to avoid being recognized. The radio description no longer corresponded to the real Nina. Yet, if they had known her true description and had searched with true love they would have found them easily. After a while the broadcasts stopped and the police began looking for other people: lunatics who had escaped from asylums, children who had run away from home. One evening, as I was on my way home, I was reminded of a letter that had been lying in my inside pocket. In the street the children were throwing stones at the metal telephone poles, and the poles rang out with each hit. Sometimes a little piece of paper in your pocket becomes more important than all the stones and metal and houses in the outside world. I opened the letter and knew where they were. They had reached the ruined crusader's castle that is near Jerusalem and is called Aqua Bella.

I went there alone. Near the road lay the charred trunk of an olive tree, and near the tree grew five red poppies. I reached the fountains near the ruin. The two of them were sitting under a tall oak tree. Their sandals lay nearby and their belts were loose—a sign that they intended to remain here for a while. I looked into their eyes with an inquisitorial gaze. First I spoke to him alone near one of the thick roots, but he didn't listen to me. His hair was smooth and had been greased with shiny oil. My words did not stay with him. Nina's hair was loose; dry oak leaves and flying thorn seeds clung to it. Her hair was open, and my words clung to her heart. I sat opposite her in the arch of the ruined window over the fountain. Nina didn't look too happy. Vagabonding was not good for her. Her eyes were too wide. She had not slept. Questions and replies played about her eyes and mouth and ears and in her anxious sleep; there were few answers in her mouth. The night came and devoured us like the wolf in the fairy tale.

The next day Nina returned to her husband, Shemuel. Shemuel wrote me that she had returned, that one morning she was standing in front of his door, that he had bathed her and put her to bed and that she slept fourteen full hours. I wanted to write him that he must leave Ashkelon because it was a bad place for both of them. Once, as I rode in a darkened bus, I thought I heard Nina's voice. I turned around and no one was there, but it seemed to me that I caught a glimpse of her bright dress and of a white strap shining over her collarbone. Maybe her dress had fallen down over her shoulder, revealing the straps of her brassiere.

Autumn arrived soon after and the clock had to be turned back an hour. All my friends looked forward to the night when they would win a free hour of anarchy, an extra hour of life. For some reason I was afraid of that hour as of an unhealthy growth on the body—a terrible hour of luxury, of Ashkelon. I awoke a bit before the moment when the clock was to be set back. I stood next to the window. Cries for help filled the vacuum of the night, like distress signals from ships at sea. I rolled up my thoughts as if to put them in an empty bottle and set them loose on the wide sea.

At that hour there came a knock on Nina's window. The Roman stood outside, white, smooth, and wonderful like the statue of a god. She followed him to that terrible thicket. There they sat on the trunk of that bent sycamore. Then he drew her with his kisses toward the deserted wellhouse, where the draw chain hung deep into the abyss. She guessed his intention and began to struggle. But he, who had been trained to wrestle from his youth and was nude and greased with wrestler's oil, only laughed. He lifted her and her arms flew upward, as in the ancient sculptures depicting the rape of helpless women. Then he dropped her into the abyss.

The extra hour passed and I closed the window. Next day the radio again began to request help in finding Nina. She had last been seen wearing a white nightgown in the manner of a Greek goddess. After a few days these broadcasts stopped too.

I forgot Nina. But sometimes, I remember her well. First I see her head, then her whole body, her elastic, brown

Mediterranean body. They say that sailors first discovered the world was round when they noticed that only the top of a mountain was visible from afar at sea, but that as they approached land, the entire mountain loomed into view. So does Nina rise in the horizon of my memory. First her head, then her entire body. Then I know, like those sailors, that my life too never rests, but revolves and revolves without end.

Translated by Ada Hameirit-Sarell

DICKY'S
DEATH

I ran hand in hand with the girl over the trenches and into the ditches. In coming days, pipeline would be laid in them. But now we ran there. The sea was far away, recurrent only in the Negev's dreams. We ran to where music was playing. It wasn't easy to make progress: a leap here, a pit there, a turned foot—and the oncoming night would make it harder on us. Dicky, close to us, walked surefooted and silent, like a ship with fine-tuned radar. He had walked through enemy lines to see his newborn daughter.

Why did we run, the girl and I, on that day of cease-fire in a Negev surrounded by enemies, cut off from the north and from the sea? We wanted to get to the half-ruined house from which the melody of Schubert's quartet was drifting. *Death and the Maiden*—the two of them, like us, at large in the world. We were young blood, and the whole land was old, its vessels plugged and valved. Sighs left for the sea and for the wide sky, and winds blew; but the roads were blocked, and rocks obstructed the trails. Schubert and his musicians sat doubled over in the wooden box of the radio in the ruined house near the ditches: Without kids like us skipping around in the old land, blood in its veins, the land would have ceased existing.

That summer the earth sprouted wire fences. What else did it yield in that fallow year? Aftergrowth of blood, and remnants of harvest for fate to glean casually. We set out for the crumbling hut to connect with the world. Since then I haven't returned to the sorghum farm in the South. I've heard *Death and the Maiden* often, just as I've witnessed death and seen maidens—and one or two of them have been mine. (Dicky's daughter would also be a maiden linked with death.) I always said that I would go back to the sorghum fields, visit the hill and white wadi. But there was never enough peace in the country for me to return to reminisce in the places of war.

The Ashdod sands blow around and find their way to my sleep, and my sleep is heavy many nights. The girl and I, returning from listening to the quartet, didn't run anymore. Our ears were full of melody, like my shoes when I was a boy and had stepped in a puddle and was happy. Our ears were heavy then, when barbed wire was in bloom and meager cease-fire weeds sprouted among the rocks of destruction.

Dicky walked alone. At night he went up from the Negev alone, between the enemy hills. All of us—the enemy and we ourselves—were terrible children who killed each other in our childishness. Dicky was the only mature one among us, and he went, two days before his death, to see his newborn. He got up and said: "Tonight I'm going

north to Givat Brenner." Angel-like airplanes came more
frequently that last day of the truce and brought many
things. White, airplane-like angels landed near the heart,
near the grove, in the wadi, between fulfillment and longing, not far from the young men and women.

When Dicky was wounded the following night, he kept
walking, the wound in his chest. In fact, he hasn't stopped
walking, and now there is another man in the world who
goes around yelling. Maybe he's yelling at us to sit down
at the table; maybe he's yelling about the cleanliness of the
battalion; maybe he's yelling wordless syllables, understand-
able universally and in every language. Maybe he's yelling
because he's so adult and big, already a bull in the world,
a fertile bull in the world, with big, serious eyes.

At first, when the battalion was organized, I wasn't in
Dicky's company. We made camp at the Okavah razor-blade
factory near Rishon-Letsiyon, and did our target practice
on the wall of the cemetery, shooting eastward in the direction of Sarafand. Only later were we crouching in the
wadi near kibbutz Ruhama. "Negev-rats" walked around
there negligently, wearing their wide-brimmed hats. Colo-
nel Marcus came and said: "Where are the reinforcements?"
They pointed to us young men and women. He said to one
of his entourage: "These are scouts out on a hike!" Some
of the scouts later hiked to distant places from which there
is no coming back, or tied knots that can't be untied.

Almost every evening we would go out on small actions. In the afternoon jeeps pulled up; in them sat "those-
in-the-know." I didn't envy them their military rank, but
I did envy their knowledge of what would happen during
the night, for we didn't know. We stood on the hill at
Ruhama. The girls accompanied us to the mouth of the
wadi, like in an opera, the consorts of brigands. In the
morning we returned; once we returned with dead. Those-

in-the-know made a speech before the ranks, and we got into the trucks. One truck was the property of the Yizhar Oil Company and had a kind of canopy over it on which the names of Yizhar's products were written. On the road this cloth flapped, the boy's death canopy. By the abandoned well at the bend in the road, one truck always overturned. We burned villages, we set fields on fire, shooed animals from their stalls. We didn't know what we were doing. In the morning, as I said, we returned to Ruhama. We burned villages and the girls burned the food. We ate it anyway.

It was then that I heard Dicky's name for the first time. Dicky-Company. I didn't know what he looked like. Today in the army, you meet the officers before you meet your fellow soldiers. Then it wasn't so. I pictured him as tall, English-looking, with a blond moustache. Then I saw him: a short, compact man with eyes that were sure and fatherly. When the truce was declared they took me to Dicky's unit; they told me to be his aide in company matters. To this day, I don't know why he chose me. I wasn't one of the veterans of the Palmach, having joined its ranks only at the outbreak of the war. Maybe because we were both from Germany; or because I had been in the British army and he hoped that I would introduce improvements into the life of the unit—as in matters of hygiene, or the procedure for digging holes. How, say, was the call of nature being handled?

In the sorghum field on the other side of the white wadi we used to advance across a long exposed front, boys and girls separately. We would advance that way to the horizon. I loved to sit at the horizon's edge and meditate; we were living like the other small animals. There was no harm in it. I took up residence in Dicky's tent, our command post, on a crate containing a card file that resembled less a box of military records than the card catalogue of a school library. Little Hanka with the beautiful hair was in charge of the file. Every evening she took the lamp and went to sleep in the clay hut standing in the vineyard, like one of those elves that go down under the ground. Her face would engage the lamp in dialogue:

"My light becomes you."

"I am the spirit of light. I am the moon."

"Off. Off in a puff, and I'm off."

"Go back to Dicky's tent."

"Your face is sleeping. I must return."

Dicky loved educating Hanka and all the trainees. Like a father, he would teach them not to yell, to be clean and decent, how to dine politely, and how to die quietly.

I stayed with Dicky in the dark. During the truce he told me about his wife who was about to give birth. The big grapes had come out in the wadi; wherever you extended your hand, you touched a bunch. The grapes were good, especially since they weren't being tended, abandoned like the young men and women. But even they sweetened. We used to talk a lot during those nights of quiet—about the days of Youth Aliyah, and about the issue of kibbutzim. Here and there a word fell in German. The shafts of grain whispered in the stalks. The moon did what it's supposed to do. Everyone did what they were supposed to do. What were we looking for, what were we feeling, what did we desire in the white sand, that sometimes tested us to see if we were fit for it? If not for Dicky, I would have been alone during those days of cease-fire. My thoughts were like a ball rebounding from the wall to the hands of the players. I was still busy with things in the past, letters that had ceased being written. My eyes looked inward, checking on my fortified heart, the ditches of my blood, the trenches of my flesh. I happened to hear Dicky's words, but I didn't know where the girls slept at night. I saw them disappear among the vines and I heard their names being called. Sometimes I went to the kibbutz, as I did on hearing Schubert's quartet. There were many reasons. In the evenings campfires burned and Dicky had his daughter in his wife's belly and the white sand tried to go to the severed sea.

One morning I got up early. There was singing, and I thought that the sea had come to us. Then I saw that reinforcements were arriving. The road dipped behind a chain of hills and I saw only the heads of those coming. And they were singing.

Then the Negev was sealed off again, as after a difficult birth. Sometimes villages still burned. I don't know if we had a flag, just like I don't remember what I discussed with Dicky. Maybe we reminisced about other evenings. Sometimes you could see lizard tracks in the soft sand. That's how we kept our spirits up. Sometimes an airplane came. It's possible that I once said that we were like bulls waiting to enter the ring. We received mail—characters on sheets of paper: in the North life arranged itself. When we spoke, the words were as tired as a battalion that has walked all night around the enemy flank to attack. One time clothing arrived, a partly starched gray cloth that tore right away. Or they sent sacks of women's underwear to the men's unit.

Two days before the end of the cease-fire Dicky set out for the North. He went to see what would be left after his death; he no longer belonged to the land of the living, and was already looking over the wall. He must have touched the infant's cheek with his finger—and found neither death nor a maiden, but only the small baby. On the following night, he returned and immediately began planning the maneuver. The company was divided in half. One group headed for a certain place, and the other group, led by Dicky, headed for another. The group that left with Dicky went out to die on every high hill and under every spreading tree. He was not wrong in going to the baby. This time he ran among the hills and fell into a trap—and walked out of it, as he still walks out every night. But he is dead. Nowadays, when there is a military action, press photographers go along. What did Dicky photograph with his courageous eyes, and who developed what he saw?

Hanka waited; Dicky was like a father to her. In the evening she didn't return to the hut, but waited with all of us in the tent. They said that henceforth Dicky and those with him would be considered missing; maybe he was captured. Hanka was silent, and so was her beautiful hair. Several days later the battalion was split during our failed raid on the fort at Irāq Suwaydāh in the enemy corridor. Most of the battalion was left in the north. The dead were left here and there. Exhibits often have charts with small bulbs that are on or off. If the battalion had been made into an exhibit, the bulbs would have been replaced with those fallen dead.

During one of the truces, men in the Givati brigade told us that a mass grave had been found near Ḥulayqāt, called Ḥeletz today. We set out, some of us having known Dicky from the South; and members of Givat Brenner met us there. We were outfitted with shovels and all the other tools of excavation to unearth the bodies. Today everyone takes up archeology. Every child knows something about the Dead Sea Scrolls and the digs at Beit-She'arim. What we excavated then was not archaeological, and not for the sake of the past nor for the future, not for purposes of restoration, not even so that we could cry. Some worked on the mound, some stood on the side quietly. The dry wintry air broke any words that were spoken.

Then we returned north and south. The Negev was no longer cut off. Only the dead were cut off, and those still living. The missing became the dead, and the dead were missing from the world and then too from our thoughts. Returning to the camp we went through quite a few road-blocks. They examined our papers. I envied the sentry who asked us, "Where are you coming from?" and got a clear answer. When we're standing between Where-from and Where-to, we won't know how to put the question. And no one will pass; no one will answer. At night I lay on the ground, putting my ear to it, the way you might put your ear to railroad tracks to hear if the train is coming. O what I needed to hear, and what I never heard.

Later, when we were in the North, I went to Givat Brenner. Dicky's duffel bag had been left in his tent. Hanka and her beautiful hair were on leave, and I took the bag. As I left camp, new recruits were arriving with their new duffel bags in hand. I passed close to them with Dicky's bag in mine. I reached Givat Brenner and entered the main office; they led me to the infirmary. I left the bag in the smell of the infirmary and went to Dicky's wife, over near the flowers and in the bungalow. I hadn't said a word when she started to comfort me and distract my attention: "The factory's expanded . . ." (that is, did he suffer much when he died?); "I believe in education . . ." (which is to say, shrapnel tore open his chest); "The plans are to have the farm extend to the side of the wadi . . ." (meaning, what was he thinking about at the last moment?). Now there is another man who walks around yelling in the world. All the tomes of history will not shut his mouth or his wound. According to my watch, he should be coming through to-night. He has laws like the stars.

We went to the infants' house. Beneath the nets were four babies; one was his. She was tranquil, a finger in her mouth. God, give us grown-ups a finger like that too.

There were more battles and more truces. Once I was

YEHUDA AMICHAI

standing with my girl and cannons rolled by us quietly. If they had been noisy, they wouldn't have been as frightening as the slight, quiet guns that passed through our city where we made love. Once in the spring we were embracing beside a tank that was standing with its treads dismantled. My girl was with me and, like that tank, I had already become unused to thinking about the war.

The war ended like a bus stopping slowly. It stopped so quietly that we didn't even fall slightly forward, as happens on a stopping bus.

We scattered like paper after an election, to every region. Only the dead were cast in the dark ballot box, only they had influenced what was to be. We who flew—the designating letters that were so clear, blurred on us. A few thought they were fleeing their duty, their orders, and to this day they live in the dark fish-belly, like Jonah; only sometimes the belly is lit electrically. So it happened to each and every one of us.

As for the living, one may conclude with the closing formula of legends: "And if they haven't died, they are living still." As for the dead, and as for Dicky, one must write: "And if they haven't risen to life, they are still dead."

And that seems to be the case.

Translated by Elinor Grumet

THE
ORGY

Yesterday was Yom Kippur. Not that I fasted, not that I
went to shul, but I did take a look in from the synagogue
entrance. The entrance was narrow, but the splendor inside
was expansive, its edges dissolved in an aura of light and
talis-and-yarmulka whiteness. I stood next to the black
doorman, who invited me to enter as you might invite some
curious person to enter an expensive nightclub. The ache
of living in a place far from my home stirred in me again.
Or, more accurately, I should say an ache's approximation.
The tortures of foreignness had been subdued in me for
some time, only to become a scraping and tapping in my
bowels—infiltrating even the joys of my dick on nights
of love. Anyway, that organ began to be selfish. It kept
the sweetness of its affairs to itself, without sharing

that sweetness, as it did when I was younger, with the rest of my body.

It is written: "And you shall afflict your souls." It is *not* written: "And you shall afflict your bodies." As far as afflicting my soul was concerned, all year had been Yom Kippur for me. If I would afflict my body by fasting and standing all day in shul, I wouldn't be able to fulfill the commandment of afflicting my soul. Why? Because only food can strengthen the body for full sensual awareness of the affliction of its soul. A felon who is sick and wounded is always, first very diligently and mercifully, healed in a hospital before being tried and judged. I was already propounding these incisively logical arguments to myself as I walked back to my dark apartment on Seventy-sixth Street, which takes its darkness and sadness from Columbus Avenue and Amsterdam Avenue—lying between them.

These logical conversations are helpful exercises for my fatigued brain. My teachers at the university in Jerusalem promised me a great future that would begin the very moment I laid down my pen at the last stroke of the last word of my dissertation. I've dreamed about that elaborate flourish more than once. But this same passion for logic set itself like a golem against the completion of my doctorate. At that dangerous stage, my teachers turned into fathers and doctors and sent me to the United States for a "change of climate," as they put it so kindly. A person will do many things to pull himself out of a hole. My method is to say, This is not a dissertation I am writing, I'm not obligated to do it, this is not my city, not my apartment, and, in sum, this is not me. And as a result of all this, the not-I will be able to do the not-work.

I washed out a couple of my T-shirts and shorts and hung them to dry in the narrow bathtub. He who does his laundry on Yom Kippur does an act of atonement. ("Though your sins be scarlet, they shall be white as snow.") Whenever my underwear is white, I reason, I'm pure as a babe. But now come women—and even men—wearing underwear blazing in all colors of sin. And thus begins the destruction of the distinction between inner and outer, between soul and body. I well know that my generation is among the last to speak of them separately. It's a habit that's captured even distinguished physicists returning from their polished laboratories in the evening, who will see the sky and say, "The sun is setting." So I continue to talk about my body and about my soul: the former is tired while the latter is full of pep, or vice versa. My body refreshes itself with sleep, while my soul is awake being crushed in its factory of good and bad dreams. Another game.

Meanwhile my clothes were dripping into the tub, and the beats got fainter, as if they were so many hearts holding back my life. I sat in the red armchair. It didn't turn white. It was remembering all the dirty things I'd done in it and couldn't forget. Overhead, in the apartment above me, they were moving the furniture around as usual. I listened to scraping and dragging and sweeping. Heavy things were being moved around light things, and the light things hid from them, with hovering, fluttering wings. This was my heaven: pounding steps engulfing soft steps. Bodies and souls in an eternal game of tag. The tittering of angels and the hoofing of goats.

In the early afternoon, about the time of *Mincha*, I went down to Lower Manhattan to see the ships. "Get ye to the harbor, sad one" (from my private book of proverbs). The ships stood dwarfed by the skyscrapers. I read their names like prayers; I forget my own name—one link in a chain of forgettings. Also, I couldn't tell you the names of places where I happen to be. As in a war when they designate a place by code, the place becomes a nonplace, and life not-life. I walked from ship to ship. Some had the names of fruits. The bridges, taut and hovering over me, swelled a happiness in me to tears, and I felt comforted. I granted myself atonement. Ships are the angels in a generation that refuses to be either angels or prophets. The possibility of sailing out, and the sweet weakness of not-sailing, excited me, till I sang out, "Open us a gate even as the gate swings closed!" into the noise of the harbor.

With the coming of evening, I returned to my dim rooms. My underwear—that soul of my body—was already dry. I folded it with the attentiveness and precision of a solitary man. I was a proud exile, filled with grief. I prepared myself a big meal, proper for those afflicting themselves on the evening after Yom Kippur. I opened a can of pineapple and drank wine grown and bottled in Zichron Ya'akov.

That very evening the possibility of a real orgy became apparent. A telephone call and a visit from a friend or two brought the news.

But later on, hope of the event we all longed for again dimmed. For more than a few years we had been talking about it, but we had never managed to pull it off. At eleven o'clock, one of my friends quoted me some lines from a well-known poet over the phone:

A LAMENTATION ON THE ROYAL COMMISSIONER LAO-SOHN

The orgy went on, moving Eastward.
But we, unfortunately, moved on to the West.

The next morning the possibility again began to take shape. For a few days—from Yom Kippur to Hoshanah Rabba—hope thickened. Sam Abend, Steve, Maude, Maggie, Malkah, Janet, Bob, and Tim the architect almost achieved a close and facilitating contact. The need to pass through the shared carnal experience to something sublime and spiritual was so great that a heavy depression fell on all of us. We hoped secretly in our hearts that this depression was nothing other than the tight coils of our will that were destined to unspring and leap into act. The great possibility of realizing my terrible longing for a different life, to live with others, to be the others themselves, didn't stop troubling me. But by Simchas Torah the possibility of the orgy seemed to disperse like clouds that would never yield rain. Then suddenly, the day after Simchas Torah, our big chance came.

2

Those same autumn days all my friends were busy with the death of God—with His death and the chances of His living, with His existence and His nonexistence, with the invention of His being and the invention of His death. Many intellectuals were going around to different universities to debate publicly everything connected with the death of God. Steve, my intimate and enemy, was one of those actively involved. An Orthodox rabbi turned professor of philosophy, he handled the discussions with great panache; and that evening after Simchas Torah, the hall in which he spoke was crowded and hot, while outside the cold had already emptied the streets. I still sat in the audience, but with little doubt that in a short time I would be sitting with the debaters on stage. The auditorium was paneled in expensive wood—the silent rustle of Canadian forests transmogrified to a lecture hall.

Steve sat behind a flashing pitcher of water, while his opponent, a Protestant theologian, spoke through the mike. His face was pink and his hair white; he spoke about the Lord, the incarnation of Love and the Good, Life Omnipresent, and about childhood. I loved the man because he had the audacity to be simple and warm. The good minister added that God sometimes hides Himself so that we shall have to seek Him. And I chimed in—in my heart because I never dared use my mouth: God shows a dead face so that we'll busy ourselves with His resurrection. And by all this wrenching of heart, and labor of soul, and anguished fussing around His bier, everyone will be busying himself with Him, so He'll live forever. He's a God who's inclined to regular dying, so the menace of His death perpetually hangs over us. By way of contrast to what I'd said in my heart, Maude, who was sitting next to me, answered in hers: I know He's dead. His death poisons the universe. His corpse is huge, and it's impossible to turn it away from the earth, and there isn't enough room in the ground to bury it. To this my hand remarked to hers, touching it: We are the honey in the carcass of the lion. Her knee, which pressed against my knee, continued on its own with the wisdom of knees: We live in a carcass like creeping worms. My tongue (now cleaving to my palate from all the honey) whispered: Life is like a giant cheese, a confusion of holes and tunnels and openings. With that we ended our body chat. The chairman of the panel, a Jew resembling a hawk, gave the floor to Steve. And Steve, my intimate and sweet enemy, looked even more handsome than usual. A big curl going a little silver made his face like a window from which his mischievous eyes looked out; his face was the face of a clever boy.

Maude sat tense and full of desire. Certainly her heart was torn between me and him. Certainly she was again making comparisons. It was a good thing she was dressed in a dark suit; otherwise you would have been able to see the marks of passion on her skin, and smell that smell of hers—of a waking animal.

Steve was dressed in the most elegant Madison Avenue fashion, his white hands shooting out of the sleeves of his blue velvet jacket. Without saying a word, he began to cover the blackboard behind the table with Latin and Greek letters and weird mathematical symbols: the Signs and Manifestations of men of science. Then he began to explain everything in a voice that still had something of Talmudic singsong in it. First he proved that God is alive and well. Using exactly the same symbols, he proved that He is dead. And with still the same symbols, he then proved that there is no contradiction between the two.

A great flame of envy rose from my neck at the thought that these were the same logical strategies with which he forestalled all possibility that Maude would object to taking her clothes off.

Being a logician herself, she couldn't help yielding to the same mode of argument. All women are naked under their clothes. Correct. If all women are, then you must be too. Ergo, a complete woman is a naked woman. Let us assign her the letter "a"; let all her articles of clothing be given other letters as needed. Granted. It is possible, then, to write thus: $a = a - (b + c + d)$. This equation is good only in the summer. In the wintertime you have to add letters for nylons, garter belts, undershirts, thermal underwear, and the like: $a = a - (b + c + d + e + f + g)$.

In the bedroom of Steve's apartment a blackboard is hanging over the bed. At the place on the wall where other people hang a romantic picture or a mirror so they can see themselves in their passion—and thus be objective observers of the subjective act—Steve has a schoolroom blackboard, and the multicolored chalk dust sometimes gets mixed with sweat and curly hairs. Steve's logical power is like the power of a vortex or a Moloch. In a strange way and despite myself, I am drawn to such types. That's how I lost Malkah, the Israeli gym teacher who's now attached herself to our group of intellectuals. That's also how my longing body lost Maude. They come back to me different and strange, as after some terrible process. Steve calls these round-robin swappings an orgy with a slow beat, a stuttering orgy, a crawling orgy.

Malkah sat four rows behind us. Maude spotted her and waved her hand in that intimate code that women have among themselves, especially women who've slept with the same man. And when I turned around to Malkah, I wasn't myself but an allusive wave, an incidental, a sad and gentle gesture. On stage, Steve was speaking about the concept of God's concealed face and the significance of its inherent death. There's a lot of face-concealing in my life—and it's like a solar eclipse. Malkah's eyes were calm and satisfied because she'd satisfied a lot of love; after intermission I sat down next to her. Her skin was still the skin she acquired on the beaches of Herzliah. She was a popular beach bunny in her time, and everyone who ran after her bruised first his feet and then his heart. The freckles on her face and body were red stars in the daytime and black at night. Malkah said whispered, pacifying things to me about faulty elevators that went up and down and skipped floors and got all messed up and that's why we didn't meet that night at the college when I got lost in the ballet department looking for her.

The hawk man on stage was erasing Steve's symbols with wide-arched black strokes, like a boy sketching in the high heavens. He began his remarks by criticizing Steve, and the theologian was happy, with a light in his eye. But suddenly that quick logical kink hit him, and in a few seconds the good man's plumes of childlikeness were plucked and all his sedating angels had flown. "This is like a rape with the tattered clothes flying all around," Malkah whispered to me. Then Maude got up, walked down the aisle, and very charmingly went up the wooden stairs at the side of the stage. She was wearing flared black pants and a black jacket that fanned out below the hips, like the costume of a lady lawyer in some ballet about a terrible trial: a high-styled Portia in *The Merchant of Venice*. She said wondrous things: All mankind but myself—*they* are God. They determine my destiny and my environment.

I said to Malkah, "All mankind but myself are objects of somebody's love. But not me." And I sang her my own "Adir Hu": "Mighty is He, sad is He, who shall establish His house soo-on." Here Malkah said, "That's you, all right. You're sad, and you'll build your house soon, but it won't be mighty. It'll be pretty sad." I continued my line: "Mighty is He, a woman is He." Malkah smiled: "Again you want to be me. You've already tried to switch with my body; you entered me—but only a little part of you penetrated. You'll never be able to be me or anybody else. And that's what's so sad about you."

The symposium ended. It was cold outside. We stood around until the whole group got itself together. The cold cut like knives. The debate continued out on the sidewalk, and I heard two opinions on a cold night. While listening to one, I stuck my left hand in my left pants pocket. After that I listened to the rebuttal and stuck my other hand in my right pocket. Meanwhile the left one had warmed up and I could take it out, ready for the next opinion. Instead I gazed around. I watched the lighted windows hidden behind venetian blinds. The slits of light cut painfully into my aching heart. Steve said in his soft, lilting voice, "Coming up with three or four opinions after an evening's debate is absolute proof that a man needs three or four women." And he went on educing evidence from the second day of yontif in the Diaspora: "It was ancient *doubt* about fixing the precise time of a festival that led to the establishment of a second day. Similarly, doubt about fixing one precise love obligates a man to have a couple of lovers at the very same time." The others' voices hushed, and the possibility of an orgy reared itself again. The people standing out in the cold looked around at each other to see who was with them.

It was midnight. We made little progress, and didn't know where we were going. We found ourselves standing outside the women's detention center. A man stood next to us on the sidewalk and shouted something, his head raised like a wailing jackal. On the fifth floor, you could see the distant face of a woman behind the bars. The transfer of inmates from jail to jail was made in the early hours after midnight. It's the same with me. Whoever wants to love me will have to rescue me boldly, like in the Middle Ages. With my luck, who'd get the ransom money but that bitch Black Solitude! My past commandeers all the dazzling coins, and still can't get enough.

Meanwhile, somebody brought out a couple of bottles of liquor. No one spoke for fear speech would make the orgy bloom. Maude had a place on a street in the Village that curved around like a ram's horn. Going up the wooden steps, we began to pair off. Redheaded Sam Abend—another enemy of Steve's and mine—attached himself to Malkah. It was as if his freckles were pulled, freckle to freckle, to those of Malkah, like bolts. I tried to displace their closeness but couldn't. Taking off our overcoats—some were wool, some other animals' skins—turned into a strange rite of coupling and mixing; and the big soft pile on one of the beds was redolent of mixed human and animal smells. A black coat was entwined with the woolly sleeves of a white coat. There was a pause. It was as if our taking off our coats was a substitute for the expected orgy. Things didn't flow.

If a couple of people had continued to take off the rest of their clothes, dream possessed, we would have been closer to our goal. Sam Abend tried to salvage what there was to salvage. He embraced Malkah the gym teacher and sat her on his lap, while we all sat around them. What is a Modern Woman? She's one who doesn't mind taking her clothes off in front of her friends. In the Garden of Eden they were ashamed because they ate from the Tree of Knowledge and were afraid of God. If God is dead, who's there to be embarrassed in front of? Anyway, some woman has to start it.

Malkah: "Why me?" "Because you were an officer in the Israeli Defense Forces and you were fearless and because you're strong and can use your powerful legs to kick anybody who comes near you that you don't want." Maude tried to pull Malkah's dress off, but Malkah pushed her and she fell sprawling out on the carpet, to everyone's delight. What is a Modern Woman? She's dead, like God. Afterward, when all those assembled had despaired, Malkah started to take off her dress. She did it with an indifferent pull of her shoulders, her lips pursed in contempt and boredom. She finished, remaining dressed only in her black underwear, and when no man moved—the confusion and yearning were so great—she knelt like a bridge on the rug. And a perfect bridge it was; her phys ed teacher's body was perfect, and her thighs were brown and full. Everyone remarked on the bridge and on the beauty of her body, and she was in the center, her wonderful body taut with absolute contempt for all the orgiasts. Only Sam Abend tried to pick her up as she was, but couldn't make it. Someone asked, "What about everybody else?" Sam Abend knelt as if by a spring and kissed her navel. Then Malkah got up and the two of them disappeared into the bathroom, where they filled the tub with all the blankets and towels and dirty laundry and did their thing, privately. Maude gave me one of her lover's cigars and lit it with a lighter that another lover forgot behind the bed. Maude is rich. Her parents, who are separated, send her money. Their money's mingling in their daughter is the only connection left between the couple.

I smoked the cigar, trying to make clouds around my head. Maggie arrived. Maggie is pretty, with bright eyes. She's the assistant to the manager of an art gallery specializing in the trendy and wild, but her eyes remain calm. She lives in a small apartment designed like a toy train, with the toilet out on the landing; and whenever she goes out to answer the call of nature, the keys she uses to open the sky-blue door jingle. Somehow she was drawn into one of the maelstroms that Steve whips up in his life. After a time he invited her out to the lectures, where ideas and opinions heat up like a dust haze. Maggie was very pale—maybe from all the dust that had settled on her—but her eyes always stayed clean and bright. Before the discussions, or after them, Steve would whisper a few sweet nothings in her ear. Sometimes he even spoke to her during the lecture itself, looking at her from the stage while talking about the bearing of love on the death of God. He would say sentimental things to her, like "Someone like you makes lecturing all worth it," or "You alone are proof that God isn't dead." After the lecture she would come over to him to give her love to the man behind the eloquence. (Of an engineer, you'd say that she wanted to know the man behind the schematics; of a smoker, to know the man behind the smoke.)

Thus Steve seduced her: "You are an expert in artistic matters. Certainly you've seen the hands of Albrecht Dürer—the famous praying ones—many times." (With the next words he would place his own hands on her full thighs.) Dürer's hands are pressed against each other in the waste of self-love, but he, Steve, would pray in the spirit of communion with his fellowman. So his hands reach the baby folds of her buttocks, as he says things about the beginning being the end, and the end being the beginning, and buttocks being the projection of the thighs, and thighs being the inspiration of the ass (though it is plumper), and the nobility of the back (though it is more supple). And in his own inimitable way he asserts that neither the beginning nor the end is important—it's the middle that is the essence. Meanwhile, his fingertips have made it to that mysterious place where three meet and nearly are one: smooth and tender skin, a band of panty, and curly hair. His hands cease being prayerful and become godly. And then the two of them stop talking to follow his handicraft with an almost scientific curiosity, as if Steve and Maggie were doing something to some third person. "Note here that what is subjective becomes objective—we are both acting and observing in one and the same moment. The eyes become pure instruments of perception, as if no brain were working behind them."

Once Steve told me that women in love in his bed resembled each other like airports all over the world. Everything beyond them—their cities, landscapes, clouds, their people living out their lives—is all only so much local dressing.

Maude was talking on the phone, a fact unimportant in itself if it weren't for the momentous subject of her conversation. She lifted the receiver from the phone's base, which was shaped like a white kitten, and stretched out on the bed letting the cord follow between her legs like a snake. The whole burden of the conversation seemed to lie on her; she fondled the receiver and drank from it and gushed her words into it. A few of the guests stood around her after having tired of looking at Malkah's new bridges. Maude undulated around and completed her striptease by shaking her shoes off her feet. Sam Abend said, "That's a pretty hot conversation." No doubt at the other end of the line was a man wriggling around just like her. You could probably arrange orgies-by-telephone, the way they set up chess matches long distance. It isn't God that's dead; feeling is dead, love is dead. "Because we wanted to live painlessly we killed Pain, like an old toothache—and with it, Love." These were Maude's last words into the phone. True to form, she then stood up and fell onto our group like an exploding shell. The room was witness: the closet door crashed open, spilling sweaters and linen and blouses like entrails. One of her shoes swung from the doorknob and the smack of the door dislodged and burst open an overnight case always kept packed and ready to go: "I was born in a suitcase."

Then the women pushed the men off the wide bed— the pile of coats with them—and a clowning female organism took their place on the bed. It was a sort of many-armed and -legged machine emitting cries and naughty whispers. The men stood around, wanting to fall on this pack and wreak design and devastation upon it. But even stronger was the desire to strike into that smooth-surfaced confused mass with a stick—like a naughty kid with a stick in his hand and the need to beat up whatever looks happy to him. It was a terrible Thing of female intrigue: a stratocumulus alive with naked leg lightning and shrill giggles. Beside this glob, all the male occupations, like trucking and driving tanks and airplanes, and building hundred-story buildings, all the affairs of microscopes and stock markets and soccer—each according to its kind—seemed insubstantial, purposeless, and without effect.

Even as the general passion of the orgy reached the boiling point, it was only a skittering grace too quickly slipping, and the bundle of girls scattered. I ended up half dozing in the armchair. Steve and Maude and Maggie lay side by side on the bed without touching each other. They were arguing among themselves, their faces turned toward the ceiling, their words rising from them in three vertical columns.

"The test is whether you can get along without him."

"I feel the same way about you."

"She wants 100 percent, but I can only give 72 percent."

"She doesn't look too good, but she's happy."

"That sweet ass throws him into a blue funk."

"Bondage . . . bondage . . ."

"His fat gut is an independent and humorous intellectual."

"All women want to get laid; all men want to get laid."

"Whoever doesn't want to get laid is neither a man nor a woman."

"And so forth, and so on, et cetera." (Gabbing)

"She looks good when she's depressed."

". . . to be a hero or a coward . . ."

"It's a question of responsibility."

"My mother's angry with me."

"Because of the Greek?"

"Yeah—the Greek professor who thought he was Jesus Christ one day and decided to walk on the reservoir in Central Park."

"They took him away."

"It was disgusting. There was half-eaten food all over the floor, like when dogs eat; and it stank."

"He's always threatening me that he'll change."

"Honey, if you don't do such and such, I *will* change."

Steve slid away, but the girls pulled him back to them. Maude placed a threatening hand where his pants bulged, but Maggie snatched her hand away like a spider. They let him get up, and he got up and left the room. Maude and Maggie continued the conversation—Maude submitting Maggie's love for Steve to logical exercise.

"Would you still love him if he had only one eye?"

"Yes."

"If he was missing a hand?"

"Yes."

"How about a leg?"

"Yes."

"Missing both legs? His penis? In a wheelchair? Without ears?"

"Yes yes yes yes."

And they continued this way till all that was left of Steve was a basketful of bone and flesh chunks. Then they laughed together and, as if spotting me, said in surprise, "You have to change him like a picture on the wall." Maggie laughed and slapped her chubby knees, which had dimples like the knots in the string around a stuffed roasted veal.

Maggie's father is a minister, and Steve's father is a rabbi, and Maude's father is a dentist; and I fell into a really deep sleep. A light dream settled on me: I was on a small boat, and the boat had entered a narrow canal. Through openings in the canal's embankment, I could see a great and faraway sea between cliffs smoothly rounded like bald heads. The sea was very spread out, and there was a powerful flowing movement which couldn't be seen from north to south. And the whole current flowed through a huge gilded gate that was a glittering harp, dripping wires and swinging lightly back and forth in rhythm with the current's breathing.

When I woke up, Maude was talking about Steve's psychiatrist, who'd died two weeks ago. "I can fight an analyst who's living, but there's no remedy against a dead one."

The man who was at the other end of the telephone call came over. He was a young architect who came to rearrange Maude's furniture and hang new pictures on the walls.

Steve came back to the bed and the deliberations were resumed. Steve told a tale about a rabbi who presided over two villages and lived between them. People came to him with questions of halachah. But living between two villages, how could he give them answers?

Maude stretched out and fell asleep; her hair spilled down to the floor. The architect caressed Maggie's heavy thighs. Steve was trying again to convince her that there was nothing between him and Maude. Maggie maintained that he obviously loved her because of her fourth apartment, which was conveniently near Columbia. The architect said, "Angels don't have wings of feathers, but of plump white thighs." Maggie said, half asleep, "My time is your time." That was really a wonderful thing to say in love, and a sweet shiver covered my back. Steve said: "A woman always cares for her body with great concentration. Therefore there are no virgins. Every woman's already made love to herself."

3

From that night on, we were no longer just a group of people discussing the death of God. We included professional intellectuals like Sam Abend, Steve, Maude, and myself; and regular hangers-on like Maggie, Malkah, and the architect; and stray people who went with us from place to place, attaching themselves and falling away on the wide, smooth parkways between university and university. After a while we bought two or three small buses for mass transit, and those times we'd come to the college towns from different directions, we'd coordinate our arrival like a guerrilla army. Brilliant guitarists or saxophonists or drummers would join us and disappear the next day at those same crossroads where angels with different missions used to separate.

After the organized debates, there was always an hour of milling around and wandering off, until all of us found our way back together again at parties in apartment buildings with beautiful gardens. We also managed an orgy here and there. Good-looking young men and women—long-haired and tan—showed up and danced and then took off their clothes as in some lovely, delicate dream, and paired off before our sad eyes.

I especially loved the road trips. There was the first snow in the country, and the last snow before spring that froze yellowish around the awful factories. Once we were discussing orgy theory in a cafeteria while some trouble with our car was being repaired in a garage. One kind of orgy is to have everyone make love simultaneously in separate rooms. Sam Abend remarked that it was like a lot of bees making honey. Steve said it was more like a whorehouse. I said it was like the Septuagint translation of the Bible: seventy language experts sat in seventy rooms and all came up with exactly the same translation even though there was no contact between them. Similarly, all the lovers would love the same love in their separate sealed rooms ("I love you." "I love you back"). Maggie said that an orgy is a matter of mutual longing that has no culmination or satisfaction. There's contact—touching skin, and hair, and hands, and genitals—like the groping of blind people. And it's not important whose, so long as you don't feel lost. Desire becomes a constant touching toward only more intense desire, because we forget most of the words that are said. The first thing forgotten is the words; after that you can still feel the shape of the words, not as letters, but in their physicality as words—in the breath caught in your throat, in your heart, in your smile, in your mind. Someone'll say, "We had this profound conversation till two in the morning." Only he won't remember the words themselves, but their shape, like the shape of a corpse under a white sheet.

And that's how we traveled and talked and traveled. We put distance between ourselves and Yom Kippur, but, like the year, we approached it again. We explained that white Yom Kippur to Maude and Maggie, and the weakness that Steve and I still felt every day, three times a day, when the time came for praying. It's not a verbal thing, but a sensation of emptiness and dizziness from the hollow of a place reserved for something that's not there. That same weakness and that same disquiet attended our evening debates. Addendum to the evolution of prayer: Man has gone from sacrifice to full-throated prayer, from full-throated prayer to whispered prayer, from whispered prayer to silent prayer, from silent prayer to death.

So it happened that on one of the first days of spring we got to Princeton, city of the illustrious university. We unloaded our gear, which by that time included speaker systems, film clips, illustrations, blackboards, plastic concept models, and bizarre clothes in all the colors of the rainbow. The debate in the evening was a big success, but in comparison the orgy was a failure. Maybe it was the fatigue of spring.

I spent the night in the beautiful, spacious home of Brenda, a local intellectual, whose husband had left her to run off with some wild beauty queen from out West. A distinguished teacher of logic's canon, she hadn't had the strength to pursue the runaway couple. "I've grown used to hugging myself in my sleep." Her eyes were beautiful, her body supple, her skin dark brown and smooth as silk, even though she was already past forty. Her eyes were permanently sad. Everything symbolized distance for her: the tree outside the window, the window itself, and even the pile of her clothes on the chair by the bed. "The parts of my body," she said, "tire in different stages and my body isn't sensually coordinated. When my legs get tired, my mind is awake to its thoughts, and when my thinking tires, my belly and cunt want love." We lay down next to each other naked.

"See how the lantern light from the garden falls on the table." Brenda is known for her comments on falling light. Sunset rays and sunlight at noon, light filtered through curtains, and light broken by shadows. We talked a lot. The difference between us, we said, was the difference between going and not remaining. We are changing. We will change. After an hour, her thinking tired and her body woke up. I caressed her wonderful skin in a quiet frenzy and lay on her a long time after I had entered her. Desire takes many forms. Brenda's silky brown skin is one of them. At long last, her entire body became aroused, and afterward we again lay side by side. "We're going to hurt each other." My voice failed me.

The next morning, the group got together again. As always, we were joined by a few newcomers whom the failed orgy and its desire had attracted to us. It was a sweet, cold spring day. Brenda's light was falling on half-frozen lakes. We all drove out to the bird sanctuary at the city limits. There we got down on our stomachs, each in his own recess, and were given binoculars. The bushes were full of birds— red ones called red cardinals, and blue ones called blue jays, and all kinds of ravens doing their high, worried, and measured business on the earth. Quick, excited cries broke from the people lying in ambush in the bird lookout. ("Stalking desire.") As I spoke, I got up unnoticed. I put distance between myself and them, till their voices were lost in the cool, clear air. I got to a hill and code-named it Spring's Fortress; and I crawled around between the trees and bushes and last fall's leaves like a soldier preparing to capture the hill. An advance-guard bird broke into a solitary warning chirrup. I continued to push forward stealthily, when suddenly from a nest in a tree overhead a bunch of them broke into an automatic chirping machine—tiki-tiki-tiki—like you hear at the beginning of a battle. I was heavy moving, and wounded from longing, and tired from a night of loving the falling light. I sought cover behind a tree stump and lay down. Behind my back, the shrill caw of a sniper bird finished me off.

I remained lying on my back like the war dead. Sunlight fell on me and illustrated me with its lovely golden designs. From the corner of my eye I saw an abandoned farmhouse that had been painted red. Below it the river flowed, released from the coast, as dead men are released from our frozen necessity to go on living. I heard my friends' voices from below. Apparently they'd got up from their lairs and scattered in all directions. They dispersed, going separate ways, and I don't know if they ever got together again and were one after that.

Translated by Elinor Grumet

LOVE IN REVERSE

Jerusalem was like a woman who had loosened her hair for her lover. That is what old Jerusalem was like on the Tenth Anniversary. Before the Tenth Anniversary and its celebrations, we had not realized how long her hair was. And then long banners appeared, festooned pillars, colored streamers and heavy screens and people celebrating or preparing and rehearsing for the great joyous occasion.

Several times he, too, went out into the street, though burdened by despair, for he was still tied up in knots and heavy as a stone. If only he could untie his coiled despair it would be transformed into long tresses of joy. In the past he had tried to do so, but soon he would be caught up in the world and then he preferred to make his loose-flowing joy a coil of despair once again.

One of those evenings on which the high tide of the holiday preparations roared through the city, he left the home of friends where he had been a dinner guest. He returned home. But where was his home and what did it hold and what waited for him there? The bunch of keys in his pocket answered with a light jingle.

Groups of dancers could be seen here and there even though it was still a week or two before the great day. At the street corners platforms had been erected which reminded him of gallows from the days of the revolution, days of terrible joy. Rugs were hanging from windows, and empty lots covered with garbage and junk were hidden by cloth screens and wooden walls. The streets were becoming more and more like indoors, like a room, so that he had no desire to hurry back to his own room whose walls would remind him of his loneliness.

The evening was soft and submissive. Singing soldiers came up from the Valley of Rephaim. When they sang, their teeth gleamed in the darkness. He was drawn after the soldiers like a child and he marched in step with them. Later he left them. He went into a café and made several telephone calls. Final calls. Final arrangements. Final instructions. That's what he thought and he didn't know why. What had ended for him? What was to begin?

Perhaps this evening would bring him, like the last drowning man who is rescued, like Robinson Crusoe, to a desolate island where he would have to build a new life for himself. What would he take with him from his former life? Where is the island? Perhaps he wouldn't reach it and would drown like the others.

He paid and left. A sudden wind shook the eucalyptus tree. It seemed to him this evening that the tree was not shaking but rather that the wind which had seized the tree was shaking. He cautioned himself against illusions. He would end up like Pharaoh who pursued the people of Israel, to have the divided sea fall on him from either side.

The night was like a soft mattress into which one sinks. He did not want to return to his house and he walked around until his knees trembled. Only then did he come near the house. Suddenly, in his great weariness, a strange thought glimmered: I will be sick, I will be sick! This thought stubbornly repeated itself until it became an obsession.

He took the bunch of keys from his pocket. They seemed to him more numerous than usual tonight. Then he took out one key, as an airplane about to land lowers a pair of wheels from its belly—thus he took out his key. He could not find the light switch at the entrance. He groped in the darkened stairwell until he found the stairs and the railing. And all this time the idea that he was going to be sick did not leave him. The railing was smoother and wider than usual. What had happened to the house? How it had changed!

His fingers found the door. The house appeared to be untenanted and he smelled fresh paint. The key also sought out the lock. Quickly and with a sleepwalker's confidence the key slipped into the narrow slot. A slight turn, a small squeak—and he stood inside. He knew at once that it was not his house or his key, but since he was accustomed to living a life not his own he was not surprised and he did not ask and he did not retreat; he accepted his fate.

He shut the door quietly, but he was not able to prevent the final click from sounding. He listened, but there was no answer, for the house was empty and was filled only with great anticipation. The stillness clamped onto him. He stood motionless, breathing silently.

When he got his bearings, he realized that he was standing in a square anteroom. He took off his shoes and began to move along the walls as though he were in an ancient sepulcher filled with jewelry, and engravings upon the walls and ceiling.

Now he heard the sound of water dripping from a faucet. That faucet should be fixed! Hanging in the closet there were coats, soft and woolly and deep as all this wondrous evening; coats of a woman. A delicate fragrance of perfume assailed him. In the far distance he heard cars driving around and shifting gears. The sounds of the street seemed to have come through many walls and coats before reaching him. How could that be? He surely had not come that far inside. He surely had not sunk that far into a dream.

Suddenly he was filled with joy. The world was still alive. The tiny feather of his loneliness, which for many years had covered the mouth of the world, stirred. The world was alive. His life too had reached a turning point, just as the cars turning near the house had to shift gears. How would he get out of here? His groping fingers touched a small table made of a sheet of glass in an iron frame. There was a porcelain dish on the table. Much paper rustled in the dish, foretelling another life for him. This hurt him. Whenever he touched upon other lives he felt a stabbing in his heart. This was a disorderly pile of papers, some of them rough and some of them smooth and silky like air letters from far away. His sickness mounted. How did the key happen to be among the other keys?

Then he stood still again and listened. The dripping stopped as if holding back in anticipation. He opened the door which had been the first to submit to him and he entered the room, already feeling that the square anteroom was his birthplace. But he stayed in the new room, found an easy chair and sat in it, hoping that not a thing would change, content to rest one hand upon the other as once he had seen medieval Christian knights made of stone, lying atop their tombs. Cars drove around at a distance of many walls. Here was the end of the world and the end of all his desires. Here he would wait.

He heard the sound of a key turning in the lock. His heart also turned. The door was opened and closed softly. Then he heard the rustle of many garments, as though many whispering, rustling women filled the square anteroom. A metal object was placed on the glass table. Paper rustled. A letter was added to the pile.

He knew that it was only one woman, for he heard her footsteps; a woman dressed in many rustling clothes, with wide hips and a large head.

Another door was opened. Water was running. Soap was put down. Jewelry was placed on glass. Everything set down with a clink was also set down on his heart.

He felt that only a thin wall stood between him and a life of which he was not yet aware. If all of this had been happening on a stage, the audience sitting in darkness would already have seen both of them. Joy and anticipation arose in his heart. Everything was understood and ready; when the door to the room opened, he was standing at her side. They came into each other's arms, mouth to mouth.

Moments earlier he had renounced everything, and now he accepted everything. Everything and nothing live in strange proximity.

For a moment they stood together. Then they realized that they could not stand thus, so they went to the other room, and still they had spoken but a few syllables. The light was not turned on. They sat on the bed. There was almost no sound, and no movement was made that was not large, accepting, and final like the end of the world, and silent like this house at the edge of time. Her dress was freshly laundered and slightly starched, the fragrance of soap and of the passing breeze clung to her, and under her arms her own delicate provocative fragrance. He asked himself: What are we seeking in life? What have I sought and what have I wanted?

Then began the hurried untying and removing and putting down and throwing down. A watch was placed on a chest. Shoes and sandals dropped off with two heavy thumps and two light ones. These were the last hard sounds. Then rustling linen and blurred silk whisperings were heard. But these were already dim echoes and not from the world out of which he had come.

Once more the jingle of his keys could be heard, but not again. Thenceforth everything for him was soft and sinking, except for her protruding hip bones and except for the nipples of her breasts which were hard as thorns. She received him as her house had received him, and as had her ready body, without asking; as the sinking sun.

Afterward, too, they did not speak. Neighbors spoke instead. Suddenly he felt that the house was full of living people. The house was full because they had loved in it. Neighbors spoke and through the thin wall they heard the voices, the calming voice of a man and the questioning voice of a woman. They heard water in the walls and sometimes pipes moaned. A car and then another; all of them turning with a screech. Then came the end of the sounds at the end of the world. Her hand stretched from the bed to set the small clock, out of force of habit.

She awakened him before dawn. He at once knew everything, without wondering. He dressed quietly. The room was full of the woman's clothes, heaped like white foam. He took his watch. He examined his keys. He went out and walked down the stairs. One of the steps was broken; he would be careful next time. Once again he felt that no one lived in the house. Like one of the cars he turned the corner, a sharp screech in his heart. It was still dark and he walked home. Home? Home!

The next day he opened the mailbox and several envelopes fell into his hand: Greetings from the government of the Tenth Anniversary, and greetings from the Histadrut, and income tax, and municipal taxes, and the electric bill, and a letter from his friend who had already gone away or died. The last of the letters was a notice in which he was directed to report for duty as an orderly on the holiday, to protect the people from the parade and the parade from the people, that no vehicle should break out of the procession and run wild through the crowd. There is much confusion and disorder in the world. Because of this we need orderlies to bring order into the world. Even a day of joy and festivity is a day of tumult and confusion.

He arrived with all the other men of his unit and they received special, elegant uniforms. Military supplies were being distributed in the middle of the field. A place for headquarters had been designated amidst thorns and the smell of dried grass. The soldiers stood among the rocks and put on their uniforms, with lifting of arms and legs and gay shouts to one another, as at the resurrection.

He returned through the yard of an old-age home that was on the way. Under the mulberry tree part of his uniform and the leather straps fell from his hands, near the mulberry tree, near one old woman who smiled toothlessly. Several old men sat at the gate, waiting for *Minchah*. When he passed among them they began to whisper with the other trees. The hanging paper decorations made a noisy rustling, sharp and shrill. In contrast, the cloth screens were heavy and made no sound except muffled explosions when the wind suddenly whipped through them. The heavy rugs which were hanging from the balconies were motionless and silent. They are heavy in their joy as though in mourning. They know.

Only a few days remained before the holiday. Were it not for the assignment which had fallen upon him and the uniform which had been given to him and the straps with which he would harness himself at the holiday, he would have forgotten himself.

Did he continue going to that house at the edge of the world? Yes, he continued going there, and his wristwatch still did not help him in apportioning his time. Sometimes he thought clear words like: I deserve it, I deserve it. Or words like: Clearance sale, clearance sale. Everything must go! Nothing can remain. People always return to the same place. Even when their village has been destroyed in the roar and flame of a nearby volcano, they return to the same village. Wild animals long ago would have abandoned the doomed place, to seek out a new place.

More and more his entire body became involved in the precise and heavy activities of a dream. A dream of night has little effect upon a man. He wakes up and forgets the dream and returns to his day. A dream of night is only the activity of an outstretched hand. But a dream by day involves the entire body. The entire body is drawn along with the outstretched arm; it leaves its own course, drawn to byways which mortals have never trod.

The earth revolves. One learns this in school, though people do not sense it. But he who left to enter another world was aware of the revolving globe, and his life became insecure and full of love.

Did he continue going to that house at the edge of the world? He did continue. He let the keys decide. The key of the woman's house always won and was taken out first. The keys divided the world for him, jangling like the bell of a factory or school.

He had not planned to pass these weeks in this manner and not in the bosom of a woman at the end of the world. Many months before the holiday he had set up his own program, his own Tenth Anniversary celebration. He had wanted to take part in reunions with comrades from his division, company, and unit. To travel to battle sites. To find what was left of trenches in which he had crouched in battle. To find them and to sit in them. A child would come over from the nearby kibbutz and stare at him with questioning eyes, not knowing that here, in this pit now covered with vines, sat a soldier amid bursting shells. And he had planned to get drunk one evening with several comrades from those days and suddenly to jump up, pound on the table and shout: "Lies, lies! All the stories about the War of Liberation are nothing but lies!" And he would keep shouting, that only very few took part in actual battles and that most of the people lived at the expense of the few and that there had been neither much volunteering nor a spirit of sacrifice in the big cities. Thus he had planned to conduct himself, and not otherwise. He would walk in the streets with a proud and slightly injured look, and would not participate in any official celebration whose main organizers would be army clerks, public officials, and munitions dealers. With pride and ironic sadness would he conduct himself among the banners and the celebrants. That is how he had wanted to act.

But everything was different now. A miracle had befallen him. Life had befallen him. Every night he would sink down into this woman. Every night the cars drove around, the house awoke from its enchanted slumber, the neighbors began to talk to each other, and water sighed in the pipes. One evening he bought much wine. The two of them frequently sat in the darkness listening to all that moved without, and to all that moved within the blood. He repaired the faucet so that it no longer dripped at night; he repaired the closet door which had not shut properly; he repaired the rod of the white curtain and moved a heavy black chest from one room to another.

One night no water came from the faucet. He said that in Jerusalem this sometimes happens. And she said, "So little water under so many rocks!" Then he knew that she was not from here, that she came from far away. This was the first distinguishing mark that he noticed in her.

He frequently would see girl tourists. They would be sitting in cafés, some arranging their hair, pushing back a curl which had fallen on the smooth forehead. They would eat a roll and leave part of it on the plate. A map of the city would be on the table, along with the colored picture postcards. Sometimes, when one of them was sitting alone, she would raise her head all of a sudden and stare out through many doors and days.

For some reason it seemed to him that only such a stranger could read his life like the map in front of her. Her having come from a distance would make it possible for her to know all of his life, like a picture which people understand only from afar.

For some reason he sensed obscurely that only a strange woman could redeem him, as in ancient days when nations chose a king from a foreign land to rule over them.

But the woman of the key was not one of these strangers who had come by sea or by air. She had not arrived that way and she would not leave that way. It seemed to him that she had come from the depths of the earth to arrive at this her final home. She was a native and a stranger at one and the same time.

The feeling of sickness had not left him. He still realized that there was no end to an end or beginning to a beginning. It is doubtful that he even knew her name in those days. She did not know his name either.

He began to fear that he would be unable to hold onto his happiness. Out of the clarity which is so characteristic of the highly feverish mind it seemed to him that he was beginning to understand the terrible structure of this love. It was love in reverse, love which began in final anonymity, in sunset free of names, age and barriers, just two in the darkness. Love such as this could not wax, it could only wane. After the silent nights there would be days of seeing each other. They would know each other's name, and then there would be strolls together, walking arm in arm at twilight, kisses followed by caresses. And then less frequent meetings would be followed by chance meetings, and then letters and after them a few letters and after them that one lone letter which is the last or the first, had this been love in the proper order. And finally oblivion once more, only not as it was those first nights, but rather the oblivion of forgetfulness or of pre-awareness. Forgetfulness of the past and ignorance of the future are equal to the heart.

Thus he envisioned and thus he beheld his love. Love in reverse order. Once he wrote a letter and put it into an envelope but did not address it. He said: Let the post-office clerk send the envelope wherever he wishes.

They began to take strolls together, but it is doubtful that any of his acquaintances saw them. These only remarked that they had not seen him for a long time. At times a desire to tell everyone he knew assailed him, to tell the truth and to flaunt it in their faces. But whatever the reason they kept their distance from him until the only thing that he had left was this miracle which was melting like snow in the heat of his love.

Out of a final effort to set things in order, and dimly, he divided his life into two periods: until now and from now on. Words were added. Conversations for two. She would suddenly say "I'll tell your mother," as children say while playing. What would she tell his mother? She would tell his mother that he is sweet, that she has a sweet son. He called her big conch-shell, pink witch, mouth of the earth. And she called him my stricken deer.

Sometimes she did not complete her sentences. She would stop in the middle of a statement, leaving him hanging with a final conjunction followed by nothing. She would say something and conclude with "because . . ." or "since . . ." or "so as not to . . ."

At first he urged her to finish what she was saying; then he tried to finish it himself into a sentence. Then he neither delved into nor thought about it and he saw in these remnants a sign that she would remain with him, for she could not leave his life without finishing what she had been saying.

The holiday drew near. But he paid it no regard, for he knew what a true holiday was. The streets were filled. People were in the streets after midnight, people carrying drums and accordions after a party.

Once they passed near the square, where a loudspeaker had been set up for the coming celebrations. Then she whispered to him that she loved him. Or she told him something like that with her remote tongue. She was afraid that the loudspeaker would magnify her words, but it did not. An engineer tested it and blew into the microphone and counted slowly: One, two, three, four, like the terrible, fateful time.

To go by his reverse love, they should have been counting four, three, two, one, concluding with the beginning which is the end.

They sat at a table in a café. The waitress came over and said: Maybe you could pay now; I have to leave. And she left. The holiday drew near. In an empty shack someone was practicing on a trumpet. A car passed by, carrying a man who was weary from all the preludes to rejoicing. The number of tourists in the city had grown. The tourists looked at the two and said: This really is the land of love. She told him that in the summer she would make a cotton dress on which his likeness would be stamped, like flowers. And still he did not see her completely, for she covered his eyes and the seven years of war in his life.

One night, when he heard her strange moanings as he came in unto her, he suddenly thought again in a source of inner anguish: I deserve it! I deserve it! I deserve it! And in the quiet of afterward he said: Until now I have carried life; now my life has become independent and mature and it shall carry me.

The cars drove around and the house awoke to the sound of human voices and the sounds of water at midnight. The window was latticed, but in the years that followed he forgot and did not remember whether the window was latticed or not.

One evening, when the key again brought him to her house, she was not there. He waited and waited but she did not come. He did not hear her key turning in the lock and did not hear the tune which she sometimes would hum to herself slightly off-key, like a squint that adds charm to a woman. He remained sitting in the easy chair. He heard several shots and he felt history passing among the living, like the blind in a city of people who can see.

He asked himself: Does it hurt? Does it hurt already? And his mind was not at ease until he could respond: Yes, it really hurts—like a doctor who sometimes finds it necessary that the patient suffer pain for the sake of the diagnosis.

Then he walked about in the room, feeling the furniture with his fingers. Then he lay down on top of the carpet, like a wounded animal. But he clutched at the legs of the bed as a fugitive clutches the corners of the Temple altar. Then he took off his wristwatch and undressed and lay down on the bed. His final thought was that he was resting like chairs in a restaurant, at night, when they are placed atop tables, their legs pointing to the ceiling.

Toward morning he awoke and saw that the woman had not come to her house that night. He got up. The closet door opened as if by itself. He saw that all of her clothes were still there and he was relieved. Everything was in disarray: dresses and underclothes, stockings and sweaters, blouses and handkerchieves. The large black suitcases stood quietly against the opposite wall, and the large mirror which held her image held his face in the first dim light of the day before the holiday.

In the late noon hours all the men of the unit who had to serve as orderlies gathered at the meeting place, a side street on which only the rear of the holiday could be seen. Contrivances and scaffoldings, rolled-up banners, unopened trunks, eyebrows of men who were staring somewhere else, a tangle of electric cord, spools of barbed wire, small tents, and everything destined to be refuse the day after tomorrow, and many posters tossed in a heap, reading: *For holders of green tickets. No admittance! Stop! Entrance to platform 8. Temporary gas station*—and many other posters which had come to replace the 613 commandments that day. Soldiers ran back and forth, asking about meeting places. Three stern-looking policemen passed by on motorcycles. On both sides of the street jars of preserves were opened and thrown onto the highway. Leftovers of bread at entrances of houses had already begun to dry up and in the empty lot between the houses two men were crouching over a small fire.

In the school site designated as the meeting place, tables had been moved around in order to make room for a dormitory for the soldiers. A group of women soldiers who had also been appointed to serve as orderlies would sleep in an adjoining room. Several of them had already put down their packs, taken off their berets, and were shaking out their hair, while laughing. Some were straightening out their uniforms and pulling at their unsightly skirts which pinched their hips, and laughing. At night one of the soldiers, he of the brown eyes—it was not certain whether his eyes were brown or maybe yellow—one of the soldiers will go into the corridor and meet one of the girls and say to her: It smells of chalk here. And she will also be reminded of school days and they will go into the empty faculty room and kiss each other near the calendars, near the stuffed raven with glass eyes.

As an officer, he was not required to sleep in the schoolhouse. After he attended to his men and gave them assignments, he went down into the yard. It was filled with soldiers from other units. He went over to the faucets and drank the jet of water which rose from the inverted faucet.

He wiped the drops from his mouth and thought about the woman. Where is she now? If she is not at home, where is she? He walked past his house and heard an explosion and heard men who were standing on the rooftops shouting: Look at the green fireworks! He did not see a thing, for the tall houses hid the sky. He would not watch, and he would not get drunk, and he would not pound the tabletop with his fist, and he would not shout: Lies, lies, it's all a lie! He thought of all the things which had slipped through his hands, of the things which were in his possession and of those which were not. He saw his life as an Haftorah that is read on the Sabbath in the synagogue, which he had attended as a child. The Haftorah must contain some allusion to what is written in the portion for that day. Sometimes a slight allusion is sufficient, merely the name of a person or a place. His life was like that, with only slight, superficial hints of his true life.

Like a Hanukkah top he was spinning and spinning until he would fall, with only one letter showing, no more.

The streets were empty, for everyone had gone to see the dances and the fireworks. A final group of dancers brushed by him like ghosts and disappeared into the light. The President's car, accompanied by fearful wailing, passed by in the street, and then he was left alone. Say not that he was sad on a holiday. Say not that he was too proud to rejoice with the masses. That man who was not pulled into the light had his reasons, reasons which were strangely mingled with ten years of the state.

That night there was not even one house to which he could return. He walked to a kiosk on the corner and asked for a glass of soda. An old man served him, for all the young people had joined the celebrations. The old man said to him: "You have a secret on your mind. Wash it down." He smiled and drank and smiled again and walked away. It would have been better to stay by the lighted window of the kiosk and to continue smiling. But it was really impossible to stay there, and he continued walking. He saw that a window in the house which he had always found darkened was lit up for the first time. The woman was lying in her bed and she said to him:—Please prepare some prunes and white rice for me; I have an upset stomach. He went to the kitchen and lit the gas stove and put the pan of prunes and rice over the flame. Then he took a Dutch plate and filled it with the food and brought it to her. He thought that he was like Jacob bringing delicacies to his blind father. Thus he entered the room and served the woman lying in darkness and waited for her blind blessing. Her hair was long. Cars were not driving around and no sounds were stirred up in the house. They heard the exploding fireworks. He sat on the edge of the bed. Her hair was long and touched the ground. He knew that it was a mistake to call the floor ground. He was always very careful to speak correct Hebrew. But in the woman's room the floor was ground, earth. The earth of all life. Even when it was covered with smooth, colored tiles.

He fed her with one hand while his other hand held her hair as someone might hold a curtain open in order to look out. He took a good look: Her face was a broad expanse. Then he closed the curtain of her hair. She left a little food in the plate. He put the plate on the ground which gave the appearance of floor. Then he touched her face with the palms of his hands. When he drew them away, he saw that they were wet. He asked her why she was crying. She answered him that she was crying because she knew that he would hurt her and because she was angry that she was crying. The people came back from the fireworks and he left her. She sat up in her bed, leaning on her hands with only the upper half of her body raised. She looked at him even after he had gone. He knew that he had to leave her and go home. Were he to remain with her he would forget his love, and it would be forgotten, like a man who sets out to scale a wonderful high mountain— were he to stay atop it, his experience would lose its meaning. He must return to people and tell them about it. This night he did not dream about his comrades who had fallen in the war, as he had intended to dream. He did not dream at all, for he did not sleep. The fireworks and the dances had stopped outside—and they commenced within him.

Early in the morning he went out to carry out the assignment which he had been given. Jerusalem seemed to be tired and her hair was unkempt. The first revellers had reached the streets. One window was already decorated with the head of a small girl. His soul was like a truck full of empty bottles. They rattled because they were empty. But he knew that they would be refilled and his soul would be calm and very heavy.

Since early morning one lone man had been sitting by himself on the ancient wall near the highway. He was very thin and his face was already turned toward the route which the marchers would take in the afternoon. All that time he did not stir from his place. However, one hour before the start of the parade he suddenly disappeared. The ways of man are strange. A man abandons his place, gives it up, and others take it.

Niches and balconies were filled with girls and families and impatient card players. First-aid stations were set up. Young doctors, in white gowns, strutted among girls who had come to help the helpers. People were being pushed along through open courtyards and winding alleys, governed by the same law which applies to the flow of blood within the body and outside of it. Arguments began over places and over chairs which had been set up before daylight. The orderlies attempted to calm them down and to settle the arguments. The girl soldiers pushed their heavy hair beneath their berets and directed the people in directions which they did not want to follow.

The unit's medic came over to him and the two of them slipped away for a little while to drink a cup of coffee. They sat near the counter on high stools, their feet dangling. They spoke about the woman in the house at the edge of the world. There were no mirrors in the café; only the metal coffee maker, in which their reflections were distorted. Suddenly he asked the doctor: What do we want out of life? What are we seeking? The doctor was startled. He had studied for many years and knew how to answer a variety of questions, but who knows what people want out of life? They stirred the coffee. Then unconsciously they switched cups. They got down from the stools and each one paid for the other's coffee, for they were elated and confused on account of that woman. They were like two roses on one stem. They went out into the street. He wanted to ask the world where its weak spot was, as they had asked Samson. He felt that the powerful world was almost like a human being.

Close to parade time his friend came over, the one who had been through the wars with him. This friend hid his eyes behind dark sunglasses; the world would have a darker view of him. He was always sad. The more he succeeded the sadder he became. His sadness was his fortress and from that fortress he looked at the world through the sunglasses.

Now they sat at the edge of the sidewalk on a side street behind the wall of people that faced the parade route. They sat beside the murky still waters of the twisting, swirling festival, among barbed wire and cast-off paper and peelings. Dust covered them. His friend spoke in a hoarse voice. When he called his attention to the hoarseness of his voice, his friend answered that he was not hoarse from his own shouting, but from the shouting of the world around him. They spoke about their generation of two wars, a generation which had no time to adjust: always early, always late. He said to his friend: But we deserve it, we deserve it.—What do we deserve?—We deserve it!

Thus the two were sad as two dogs standing near a tree. Then they returned to their duties and the festival rolled on down the street.

In the evening he went to see if the woman had recovered. She had. Her eyes were slightly crossed and her lips were full and her mouth was large and almost the shape of a brick. Her head resembled the head of the Queen of Egypt, Nefrititi. Her nose was elongated and her nostrils dilated in order to breathe in his fragrance and that of the world. She said that on the next day he would suffer a total eclipse. He repaired the shutter and then he ate and drank and was silent. He would continue to live, out of habit. He would continue to live as a child continues sobbing long after the source of pain has been forgotten.

Summer arrived several days later. One morning a wagon carrying blocks of ice passed by them, and a young boy cried out in a voice to end all voices: Iceman! Iceman! Women and children came down from nearby houses. From then on those calls of Ice, Ice, were frequent because summer had suddenly come upon the city.

Sometimes while he walked alone in the street the ice wagon would silently steal up behind him and pass him by without anyone's shouting Ice. After that, this wagon became a death wagon, gray and dirty, with thin jets of liquid trickling from the corners like blood from a slain man's mouth. This was a death wagon, like the ambulances that accompany the advancing army amidst clouds of soaring dust.

The celebrations continued outside. But the house still protected them like a plaster cast. Later they would recuperate from the fracture. Which fracture? The house would be taken from them and they would leave. Where would they go? Bit by bit the enchantment of the bewitched house was undone. Talk had been stirred up in it, and not only after midnight, but during all the hours of the day and the evening; the sounds of children and the sound of heavy steps on the stairs. The balconies were filled with clothes hung out to dry. In addition, construction had begun on a new house behind the house in which they had loved and which they had thought to be the end of the world, beyond which was nothing. And the street was extended, and cars no longer turned around near the house at night.

It seemed to him that during those days at the start of the summer they had been at the shore together. But he was not sure of this, for at that time the bond of their love had already loosened and letters had already been sent, for theirs had indeed been a love in reverse.

It seemed to him that they had been at the shore, that hand in hand they had run across the sand still bereft of people, that they had run thundering like galloping horses, hair flying, to the ruins of the ancient pillars by the sea. The soles of their feet were black with pitch and they were clinging gently to each other, near the sea, where the hotels go down to the shore and fishing nets are spread out to dry.

After that they were in Jaffa or in Acco and they walked in the footsteps of children, hiding and going into the courtyard of a house; then they went inside the house and saw that the sea dwelled on the bottom floor, that it went up and down in the rooms with the motion of the waves outside.

But they did not have the blind confidence of the first silent nights, the nights of the end which for them actually was the beginning which brought them to the true end and past it.

For a man may leave a house, but the house does not leave him. He is still there, with its walls and everything that hangs on them, with its rooms and with its doors which are carefully closed, or the house expands and becomes highways on which he who left the house will walk.

The summer waxed and the celebrations were drawn out endlessly. Due to their joy, people celebrating did not have time to lift their heads before a new wave of joy came to engulf them again.

He looked at the city and at the color of its banners. He looked at the city whose costs of destruction and re-building he bore, as all its children. Sometimes he wanted to sink as she had, with prophets prophesying and flames and clouds of smoke.

He often went to the new swimming pool. When he checked his belongings and his clothes, he received a num-bered tag in exchange. It always happened that way in his life as well. He checked many things whenever he wanted to be naked and alone: loves and memories of entire days, one night, a fragment of a conversation, a feeling here, an intuition there. Sometimes he would lose the numbered tag, or he would forget where he had checked his belongings and in the end he would give up and forget about it alto-gether. Only sometimes, at night, the band on the tag would press against his hand and he would toss from side to side and would not doze off. He would turn on the light and see the number marked upon the tag and would be alarmed. Then he would doze off again, like Pharaoh, to a new and terrible dream.

And once again their love flared up as at the start. It was like a coda at the end of a symphony, that recalls the lovely themes of the beginning, before the end. Thus their love of the first nights returned, as if to prove everything and to declare: This is the way it was and it will never be this way again.

The house remained where it was. But since they had stopped loving in it, it became as blemished, bare, and mortal as any house. Did the woman stay in the house? He frequently asked himself this question, but his bunch of keys did not answer with a jingle and that small key was not drawn out again in order to solve his life, to decide for him. The ice wagon often passed him by, even in places where there were no apartment houses, and no woman carrying baskets.

The woman sat in her easy chair. The chair was deep as the clouds of heaven and red as hellfire. Where was it? Perhaps in her house. It was even possible that it was in the middle of the street, the woman sitting in it with her head leaning to one side in heavy fatigue. Her head was like fruit on a tray and her hair flowed down along the back of the chair, almost to the ground. And perhaps in the course of time people and vehicles had become accustomed to the easy chair in the middle of the street and they went around it as if it were an island, or the municipal workers put a metal plaque and a burning flare in front of her, as they do when the street is under repair.

The house remained with all the houses. Water flowed through its pipes, but love had ceased in it. The door of the woman's apartment stayed shut, but one day, on the Sabbath, in the afternoon, a commotion began behind the walls of the other apartments, a commotion of wrath and glowing fury, a commotion of vengeance, rebellion, and jealousy. The commotion steadily mounted. At first in the pipes and in the glowering stoves and within the closets and then in the hearts of the men and women who lived there. All of the terrible and devouring inquisitiveness, all the jealousy and hate which had accumulated behind the doors of the house began to boil as though inside pressure cookers and to force out a path for themselves until the windows rattled and doors quaked in their frames. How had it begun?

It is hard to know. Perhaps this began in all of the apart-ments at one and the same time according to mutual agreement in fury and jealousy. The fat squat woman who was a teacher in the school for problem children was among the first. The two lovers had never seen her but now she appeared time and again. She was standing in her kitchen when suddenly she jumped over to the door of the apartment, opened it, and listened. Since she did not hear a thing, she brought her sense of smell into play, and wrinkled her thin, sharp nose and said: Fire, Fire! She said it in a whisper as if to convince herself. Then she raised her voice slightly and said it again, Fire, Fire—and she closed her door excitedly. Then she entered the room and awakened her husband who was lying down, a newspaper covering his face like a monument over a grave. He arose from under the newspaper, revived, and he also shouted Fire, Fire! before knowing what really had happened.

"Where is the fire?"

"In the apartment of that-one, those-over-there, that-one." The husband awoke and a strange light was kindled in his eyes. He buttoned up his trousers, pulled at his shorts which had wrinkled up in back, and strode out. Thus onward strode the hunter to the forest. When all is said and done he too was a hunter.

The two burst out to the stairway. They rang at the door of the strange woman. After ringing, they began knocking, then knocking and pounding, and finally they kicked fiercely at the door.

"You still don't smell anything?"

"Smell? What?"

"The smell of fire and smoke."

The stairway began to fill up with half-dressed people dashing about. All the tenants had looked forward to this for many weeks. And now they all came: the thin man who works at the Jewish Agency and the aging bachelor and the girl holding a doll in her hand and many others.

There seemed to be more people there than lived in the house, woman and children and a great multitude. And already many shouts of Fire! and Smoke! could be heard.

"She's endangering our house!"

"We'll all die on account of her!"

"She undoubtedly didn't turn off the iron, undoubtedly didn't turn off the stove."

"Witch, tramp, hussy. She didn't turn off her heart!"

"I saw a *goy* who came to pick her up."

"A *goy* with a blond mustache? Boy! I saw plenty!"

"They sent her flowers every day. And since she wasn't in her apartment, they hung the flowers on the doorknob and the whole house is filled with flowers!"

"The flowers rotted and smelled up the place!"

"And dirtied up the house!"

"Maybe she committed suicide?"

"Maybe she ran away?"

"She is not a Jew at all!"

"Who knows, maybe she's a spy!"

"Once I saw her jump from the window, her hair streaming something awful."

"She rode a horse; she walked around in her apartment naked!"

"She rode a motorcycle, noising around on days of rest!"

"She used to hang her underwear on the line in front of husbands and boys."

"She sang after midnight!"

"She played the guitar!"

"Where is she? Where did she go?"

Because of these shouts they forgot the fire and the smell of the fire that never was. And since they already had begun, they continued storming about. The door was broken down with one blow. It sounded like an explosion.

It was not opened as it had been opened on the first night, with a slight whisper and with the turning of a thin key to the wondrous destiny of love and white clothes.

The indignants poured into the square anteroom, which filled up at once. The woman's coat was torn from the hanger, the glass table was smashed when a fat man sat on it after the exertion of the outburst. Mazel Tov! they shouted, and the splinters were trampled underfoot. Someone cut his finger. Blood flowed. Blood!

This shout was both a call to arms and battle cry. In the kitchen a bank clerk found a half-eaten apple, marked with lipstick, which aroused his lust; he left the kitchen all agog, his eyes bulging from their sockets.

"She committed suicide."

"She ran away through the latticed window."

"She didn't even clean up her room."

"Whore! Tramp! Witch!"

In her room books were ripped from the bookshelves and thrown down. Letters were torn up after they tried in vain to decipher what was written in them. Someone cried out, Call the Police! But another pointed out that it would not be wise, since they had broken into the apartment.

"It's all right to break into the apartment of a woman like this."

"It's all right to steal from a thief."

The avengers reached the bedroom.

Drawers were forced open, a mirror was cracked, a curtain fell. One woman held up a pair of dainty underpants like a tattered battle flag. The madness of snatching and throwing, of ripping silk and nylon overcame them. The ravenous hunger of their terrible lusts. Empty perfume bottles were tossed about and trampled on. A black shoe was tossed out of the latticed window through which the two had looked when they raised themselves slightly from the bed to see the tree on the hill. But the neighbors finally tired, for the small apartment appeared big to them because they had traveled immense distances in the great world of the two lovers. At last each one of them sat down. Panting mouths were open wide; closets were open wide, and empty. Conversations ceased. No shouting could be heard, and one by one they returned to their apartments by the long road which has no end. This was the end of love in the house and the end of the house.

The two who found each other in the house on the night of nights were never in it together again; they were not together anywhere. They were already immersed in the great forgetting which exists before events and after them and they awaited each other as one waits for someone still unknown, someone who lives in the burning imagination and in dreams. And they foretold their pasts and their futures, each one in his place. And they used all those short words, such as already, still, not yet, before, a little more, afterward, once—all those short words which melt in life and sweeten it or add bitterness like wormwood.

And so it happened that one day he was sitting in the garden of the King David Hotel. The Israeli flag waved in the center of the roof, the French flag to the right, and the weather instruments to the left. Opposite him stood the cypress trees which hid the Old City. In the late afternoon they began to play. A brazen lady pianist and a sad violinist came out on the balcony; but their music was scattered by the winds. What do people want out of life? He did not ask it in a loud voice, for he sat alone. They were calling people to the telephone. They called them over the loudspeaker. *"G'veret Tufel, b'vakashah l'telefon."* Or in English, *"Meester Kleinman, telefon pleez."* Sometimes someone got up after the announcement and sometimes no one got up. And it gives one something to think about how people wander and come from distant places and meet by chance. Chance gives way to destiny. Sometimes chance can choke a man. Sometimes it is possible to feel the stitching between chance and destiny. Sometimes the stitching is soft and sometimes it is hard and coarse. And then destiny again becomes chance and it ends only at the end.

The woman sat in the easy chair, turning the pages of a thick book. Every turning of a white page looked like wings trying to fly. How did she come by her slanting eyes and her elongated head? This time her long hair was piled high in thick curls atop her head.

Once more his thoughts were like two roses on one stem. And he knew that from now on there would be only letters and later empty pages and later the after-forgetting which is like the forgetting-of-before.

The switchboard operators changed. A girl with a soft, deep voice was now on duty. He wanted them to call him, too, but they did not. For him the year of celebrations had ended and with it the year of the hair undone which fell loosely to the hips. He felt that he was close to the heart of the year and he could hear it beating, more and more faintly, like retreating footsteps.

Translated by Jules Harlow

THE SNOW

The snow began in the blind and moved outward. For years the white snow had settled in the blind. Now it was out, and white: Blindness lodged everywhere, covering everything.

The world stood like railway cars during a strike, the smoke dead. A different smoke entered the young women, and they warmed themselves, and voices rose above the hopes of ashes, and the night went on white and undisturbed.

Yaakov and Tirzah prepared to visit me, and I didn't know it yet. The wind tapped at the doors of my apartment and at the doors of my spirit with a big blindman's cane. Yaakov and Tirzah arrived and rescued me for the bath.

My house is at the bottom of a slope, and Yaakov rolled

his woman all the way to me, so that she arrived in an avalanche of snow—then leaped from inside it, her face red with the air of summer and of roses. Her breath was white when she spoke. My love too is not always visible: Only when I am cold or anguished can you see it, like Tirzah's vaporous breath.

The wind knocked at the door, and we pushed the furniture aside; I extended a hand to the wind to guide it, but it hit Tirzah's face, and her black hat was blown askew. She was wearing those black pants fastened up, the kind that girls wear on cold days of merry loving. Now black is no longer the color of mourning, and there can be no other color to mourning: It is transparent; through it you can see cities and people—everthing.

The electricity was out and wires jumped on all sides, curling on the white forehead of the snow that had no thoughts beneath it.

The moon was cold, extinguished, like the monarch of a country become a republic. The letters were cold in the red mailboxes. Some tried to flap their wings, but couldn't.

The electricity stopped, and all of it entered Tirzah.

"You can write on it like a piece of paper."

"People can make love anywhere."

"It's wonderful loving in the snow."

"Sex in the snow!"

"We ran all evening."

"I rolled her."

"A snowman with no telephone."

"My warm oven-man who loves me."

That evening the steps up to my house led only down; so how did the two climb to my door? From the rooftops! The window rattled us its commentary; the bath water got cold, and the coffee deepened in seriousness in the cups.

YEHUDA AMICHAI

Yaakov and Tirzah slid down; he wanted to roll her all the way to their house in the heights of Jerusalem. But they never made it. Instead they got as far as the Valley of the Cross and remained there: In the morning people found two black, fallen telephone poles, their wires so entangled that only God knew how to unknot them. The nearest house was too far away. Another house faced the mountains where it was forbidden to go.

All night the snow lay on my sleep. And so it was when I was born. Flesh came like white snow covering my red blood, in which swam that hungry shark, my heart. My mother's cords were cut in a storm; my ears were the cups of a telephone receiver; my nose was hope setting forth; my mouth the black wound in snow when it is stepped on. And my fingers were silent, and my legs were like the beating of hammers.

A black dog of conscience barked near the field where one goes astray. The snow that lay on my sleep melted, penetrating it. I woke up and lit the snow in my room, and saw that the world was immense and inconsolable.

The snow settled heavily where the archaeologists had excavated. But that grave was accustomed to the weight of many strata. The wire fence that had been put up to protect it had rusted out some time ago. No one cuts through there except to reach the adjacent grocery store, to get to the colorful cartons. The cartons thrown into the garbage still bear illustrations of what they once contained. That's good.

I went outside and stood under a balcony near where my close friend used to live. One day he raised a sail on his violin and put out to sea. The water seeped into his violin and he cried; but he was already too far out, participant in the world like a biblical chapter, his violin filling up. Why did he go? What was he looking for? Perhaps he set out to find the horse from whose tail the bow of his fiddle had been made. He went out very far, and the horse was swift.

When he went away, they threw him a party. His eyes were heavy, having fallen to him from distant generations. He stood by the stairs and said goodbye to us. Sometimes I feel a pull in my heart; he is tied to me as mountain climbers are tied to each other. By the tug I must surmise his movements. And sometimes the tug is painful, especially during the spring. Sometimes the rope is pulled and sounds a bell, as on a bus requested to stop.

I would have liked to continue standing there, but the snow sent me under the balcony; it had turned to hail. And then, like someone who at first has difficulty speaking and says difficult things, whose words gradually soften, the hail turned again to snow. One window in the house was blocked up with rocks. One vertical pipe stopped short of the roof; there was no longer blood in it. Other red pipes entered the ground, all standing against the wall of the house like vessels bulging on the hand of an old man. I was holding onto my dead thoughts like slaughtered chickens, their heads drooped to the ground on the way home from market. A young woman lived in the old house—lived there alone. At first it was dark, then light leapt from window to window. I stood under the balcony that had been extended into the world, like someone superfluous, someone without inception.

Sisters with necklaces bustled around in the house. Brothers with bubbling hopes sang in the tub, as I had done when Yaakov and Tirzah rolled down the slope to visit me. A car pulled up, its snow chains jangling. Dr. Gordon got out, his bag in hand. His voice said, "She's a student." The driver said, "I'll wait. I'll leave the motor running." The doctor took the bag and went into the house. All the pipes filled with new blood and smoke began to rise from the house and lights flicked on like fingered piano keys. I sat in the taxi. The doctor returned and showed me his hand: "I performed an operation in that old house." His hair was curly and his eyes looked off across the Old City, and the Old City in turn looked off toward the mountains beyond the Jordan, and the mountains looked off still farther. I got out of the taxi and it drove away. The now-healthy student—who wore a man's coat . . . she draped it on a chair . . . by now she has forgotten me—was like a trumpet call in that old house. The balcony remained thrust out like the palm of a pauper.

Sated with white, I went to look at pictures in the gallery. There was no one there but me. The gatekeeper was not at the gate, and I went in free. In one painting there was a woman combing the hair of a woman combing the hair of still another woman. Where would it all end?

I heard the guard walking through the rooms. They would be closing soon; it was almost dark. My heart lay like a carpet on the vast quietness. A carpet that's been well trampled. The sound of a typewriter came from some hidden room. Surely they were making a list of those who didn't attend. Policemen in plain clothes watched me so that I wouldn't steal. I asked: "When did you acquire these paintings?" They said: "They are ours and you are ours." I wanted to know where the typewriter was. I wanted to know what was behind the paintings. I took down a picture, and saw that a bright rectangle remained on the wall, like my heart that hasn't loved in a long time and remains clear— for the sun hasn't touched it, and it's been hidden under a picture.

I looked at the inscriptions: A painting's name did not always suit it. That's how it was with the name written on my identity card, and with the snow that was inappropriate to Jerusalem.

THE SNOW
—175—

I took in the names of the painters. A date of birth, a date of death, and between them a short line. Some of the paintings showed only a date of birth and a blank space waiting on the other side for the second date. The hail beat on the glass roof; others of the plagues of Egypt were still to follow. The paintings turned themselves to the wall, and I went out to the courtyard, and saw only snow. I paid the gatekeeper, who had returned in the meantime.

The smell of pines and other trees was in the air. Many trees were broken. Every leaf was freighted with snow. So it is with me: All the words I speak are leaves, and fate, like snow, rides heavy on them. The great danger is that I will break, so I sometimes stop speaking. If I don't produce words, I won't crack with the cargo. If I am silent, the weight of the snow can't break me. If I am unloving, I am unburdened. If I have no handles, they can't catch me; I can slip from their hands, left with myself. If I refuse color, then they can't see me.

The trees were broken and their fragrance filled the air. Only now, after their breaking, is their smell good in the world, and strong.

New hail started to strafe the earth. I found shelter in the voluminous robes of a nun. There was room in her habit for another two or three people. At first she didn't feel me. Then she objected. She accepted her situation, and we walked on together in her capacious gown. She went up the steps of the old building with me and said, "Now get out. Get out of there. Why did you come to me?" I entered her room with her. Her collar was white as snow. Her room was patched up, a shell having exploded a hole in it. I asked, "Did you cause the snow? It seems to me that a nun like you made all the snow." Suddenly I knew how to speak Swedish. I told her that Swedish was a beautiful language, and so was the shell-hole through which prayers in all languages had made their exit, until the room was repaired.

On the table stood roses in a vase. They were from before the snow and had already begun to wilt. One rose was like a heart in surgery; another like a dog run over in the street. One rose was made of paper; another rose was like a bed left unmade after sleep. I saw that the nun's eyes were sad. I saw that her eyes retained in reflection the numbers she had seen in the street; they remained and her eyes saddened.

"I've learned nothing but how to die," she said. "I still wear my father's smile like a bib tied 'round an infant so it won't dirty itself."

"I stand before my life like a small boy at a kiosk. The coin in my hand held out to the shopkeeper, I see only what has been laid at the edge of the counter—and not the wonderful shelves behind him."

We went over to the small window and saw that Jerusalem was entirely white. My life speeded up. Episodes ran by and I didn't know what to say; the plot of the film advanced in a foreign language and the Hebrew translation lagged behind at the bottom of the screen.

Jews passed by with foxes on their heads, foxes from distant forests. The face of my nun was like a country with many small gardens in it. I told her that there were two seats of tiredness in my body—the soles of my feet and my eyes. They both roam a great deal without rest.

She said, "There are two seats of sadness in my body— my feet and my eyes. My little nephew Yigal once said that everything beautiful is sad."

Sometimes she spoke to me in a faraway archaic language, from some distant Bible of snow:

"Good man."

"You were pleasant to me."

"Until when will you stay with me?"

THE SNOW

—177—

Sometimes she sang and sometimes she turned from the window. The snow was laid on the heart of Jerusalem to slow the city's death by fire. Jerusalem is always burning. Things come along to delay her death, like the snow that fell this year.

After dinner we shared a smile, insufficient for both of us; when she smiled, my mouth narrowed and contracted. Her robes were scattered around the room. She was as skinny as a chicken. My nun's brother lived at the edge of the village. He was a heavyset farmer who had settled behind a heavyset wooden door in the northern part of the world. It was difficult to reach his place in the snow.

We went out for a walk. I hid myself in her robes because I was cold, and I didn't want anyone to see me walking with a nun.

Black-haired young men passed wearing shiny moon-jackets with fur collars.

The triumphal stones of the Roman Tenth Legion were covered with snow; other stones were like human hearts, scattered and silent.

The thoughts of Tel Aviv didn't arrive; red postal-thoughts stood en route. I saw Dr. Gordon's car and knew that the student in the old house was sick again.

I sat down opposite my nun. All my thoughts were on my brow, like boats pulled onto the sand when not out fishing. I looked at her head against the waning light, as if assessing a negative: It was a good picture. We couldn't keep sitting because fresh snow began to fall on us. The houses of Jerusalem stood to the side. Some of the houses would outlive their occupants, and some of the occupants would continue living after the houses—like a man who has nothing to drink, who then finds a drink but has eaten the bread, who then gets some bread. . . . People, superfluous, needing new houses, then superfluous houses needing new people, without end, without equilibrium, without respite.

We stood beside the gate of Dr. Miller, who fixes broken limbs. The world had shattered and the snow had set as a false plaster cast. When the snow melts, the fractures will again be visible. I left her then, and went down the street.

My students came sliding down the hill. Tomorrow I'll assign them the task of finding every mention of "snow" in a concordance. As the rain and snow come down from heaven and do not return there. . . . But everyone returns. A bear was killed on a snowy day. All will be silent. Sins will become white as snow, and in my mind I'll be looking in all the snowbound places. When I was a boy, there were conventional essays in honor of snow, with conventional rhetoric. "The snow sits like little white domes on the fences." "Snow covers everything like a sheet." The rhetoric sucked out all the life. Only the tears, which it was meant to absorb, it did not absorb. The world is covered with those killed—the dead, like torn socks my mother never finished mending. I almost went back to the nun.

The car with a loudspeaker attached to its engine came by and said "Everyone aside!" I made it. "Beware of the power lines!" Employees of the Electric Company tried to repair the damage. Employees of the Post Office stood down below next to poles and telephoned heaven. I saw one smiling in the middle of his conversation, as a man might smile when phoning angels. A snowman had been built around a post at the bus station, with the upright for a soul. Children had stuck eyes in it. One boy had eaten the carrot that was the golem's nose.

Cars brought aged parents. Children tumbled in the air. Students promenaded up and down the streets. The snow fell from giant textbooks. Young women were wide open with snow and shrieked as at the seashore in the summertime.

It started to rain. I stood under a tree that protected me. The rain stopped and the tree was no longer my protector, but itself dripped on me. Quiet people are a lot like that: Sometimes after everyone has gone away they will start speaking. Sometimes no one hears them. Sometimes a small boy carrying letters of a deaf man are their only witnesses. Anyone just happening by hears them. I went to a friend's. He wiped the lenses of his eyeglasses but they clouded over again. Behind the curtain of branches of a pepper tree that bowed across the street, children were playing. We didn't dare approach them because they were living in another world. Cars separated from their owners. All the words of junction were wrong, and I didn't know how to speak. In everything there was death without forgetfulness.

But I was hungry. I went into a restaurant. The waiter took my order, and then went to the far little window and repeated my order over into that concealed and distant world. I was glad because now they knew my desire over there—in that other cosmos, beyond the mountains, above the clouds. Who was out there? Solitary pilots; lost voices and prayers that returned like boomerangs to the worshipper.

I went into the university building to look at the clock. I hadn't come to learn but to observe the passing time and look over the list of those who had gotten through the tests. There is no other place in Jerusalem. Professors continued teaching under the snow, unaware that their students had gone out to play.

In came the Three Workmen of the Apocalypse. The first carried a broom, the second a spade, and the third carried his past. They walked by me and went farther on, not knowing where my nun was, even though I asked them nothing. I threw a party: My eyes celebrated before all the sad people—my spirit made my body happy with dreams and my feet danced in the snow—I came back from there and the streets were smooth with ice—walking with small steps I finally arrived at sleep. All the time it snowed I hadn't slept. The snow, like white eyelids, slept for me. The earth slept for me beneath it.

The following day, the fog came in. The snow slowly returned to the blind; it retreated under a curtain of fog, concealing the ugliness, the black wounds, the polluted streams, the corpses of trees. On the bulletin boards many death notices had been tacked up. People usually restrained themselves, and didn't die. Now, under cover of snow, they all died at once, and there was no room on the bulletin boards. I hung a sign on myself, as on a driving-school car, and they let me pass. I learned how to walk all over again, and to love and to see and to think after the snow. Thoughts seated themselves in my mind, which they took for a dining room; and they ate in an uproar.

The Three Workmen of the Apocalypse came out of the fog, looked at me and disappeared. I never saw them working. They were always wandering around looking for a good place for their fulfillment.

A young woman got off a bus. She entered the fog. She stepped out of it, closing the door of the fog, and went into a cosmetics shop. She made her purchase and stood among the fragrances; that was her place. She never left there but I heard her voice when I fell to forgetting the nun.

The tree in front of my house that we thought would break rose again, but not to its full height. It stayed half-way to its death; or rather like a mother's neck inclined to her daughter, while her son has taken off a long time ago. The children stayed in the yard, absorbed in their games.

THE SNOW
—181—

Toward evening they hollered, "Hey, Ma, throw me a sweater!" And that was just the attitude of those at prayer, who yelled up to God to throw them His blessing so they wouldn't have to go home to get it.

Many trees were in pieces on the ground. If it were Sukkot, it would have been convenient. If only we could bend down the year, like branches, so that it would touch us. This summer there will be many bonfires in the Valley of the Cross. And perhaps Yaakov and Tirzah will rise—the two who went down there after visiting me and never came back.

In one place people were moving out of their apartment. The snow surely drove them to it, the white carpet having dizzied them. The voices of the movers were hard among the remains of the soft snow:

"Now the big chest."

"Watch out! The door."

"You there, watch out!"

"Hey lady!"

There were piles of snow melting like an unmade bed. I set up a competition: Where would the last bit of snow be left? In the back yard near the trash cans among the terrible shadows where it's deserted.

The melting snow stole the little warmth for its thaw; just as all the lovers in the world expropriate the warmth of humanity around them in order to soften each other. The others are left cold.

In a distant neighborhood, nearer to the moon than my neighborhood, a little boy drowned in a pit of water covered by snow. The boy went down to collect meteorites. His shoes floated up like water lilies. At first the pit had been full of snow. Then the snow turned to water, and the water to astonishment, and astonishment became a cry—and over it all rested a layer of snow. The soles of his shoes were like two private clouds over the earth, already far away, belonging to the rest of his body way below.

He was in the pit, having perished in the final plague, the slaying of the firstborn. The hail had already come and the blood was wonderful in Tirzah's cheeks, who had been rolled over and over by her lover; the blood was in her cheeks.

The Three Workmen came and put down their three tools near the side of the pit, and spoke quietly among themselves. Then they lay down on their stomachs to pull the boy out. The shoes came out in their hands, and light flickered on in their eyes like memorial candles. Another man came by, carrying a portable stove in his buffalo horns, the stove belly a dazzling sun. The instrument was set in the snow, which melted, but it did not save the boy. Tirzah's black pants are draped on a stick, as are the rest of her clothes, cast like thoughts on a chair—thoughts a person would like to quiet. Tomorrow she'll be wearing a dress with flowers on it.

Ropes groaned, ships sailed out of the place; ships that were beside the boy's cheek set out to sea. The world was a worldful of ships, and the boy lay like an empty pier along the snow, all the ships gone. Anchors flew away like birds.

The mother came and threw cries like bombs at the boy and at the city to wake him. The Three Workmen picked up their tools and went away. A first train went by and screamed between the mountains constricting it. Any-where in Jerusalem you can hear the train coming.

Not far from there they again took up construction work that had been suspended. The great mixer turned, setting cadence to death. The gravel and cement and sand bonded together; but we, drifting, never bond to one an-other. Instead we are sent off to the farthest extremities. The house was eventually built: At first only an empty space had been there, flooded with air, and light, and from time to time birds. Then they closed it up, turned it into cubicles, chambers, in which destinies were at once constructed. Where there had been air and expanse and the rush of wings, now was the fatedness of walls—women and men, books, and illumination after midnight.

There were sales again in the shops. In the shoe store was a sign: "Single Pairs." Is there a greater contradiction than the one between "single" and "pairs"? My thoughts were as tired and closed as the solitary passengers on a last bus: one here, two there, all bundled up and silent, and the cold wind like water already breaking into the sinking ship.

So I went to a coffeehouse. The owners' crazy son sat flipping through illustrated newspapers as God must flip through the torn pages of His heart—without understanding. There was no room for me because a meeting of Hungarians was just getting under way. Hungarian words were laid out on the table. One man shed tears; a little boy played a game of marbles with them between the table legs and the legs of the Hungarians. The orations were balanced like scales, were cyclical like the seasons: An old man's spare words were followed by the blossoming eloquence of a girl. Someone came in and they all shouted "Jarousz! Jarousz!" He brandished a rolled paper like a stick, struck the table, and joy burst forth. After a while they all left. The quiet was made up of many conversations between couples. In the houses and everywhere else I saw people.

In my eyes I cleared away the big building and another building and another building, and saw the last strips of snow near the border, outside the bars of children's dreams.

Translated by Elinor Grumet

YEHUDA AMICHAI
—184—

THE TIMES MY FATHER DIED

One Yom Kippur my father stood in front of me in synagogue. I climbed up onto the seat to get a better view of
him from the back. His neck is much easier to remember
than his face. His neck is always fixed and unchanging; but
his face is constantly in motion as he speaks, his mouth
gaping like the doorway of a dark house or like a fluttering
flag. Butterfly eyes, or eyes like postage stamps affixed to
the letter of his face, which is always mailed to faraway
places. Or his ears, which are like sails on the sea of his
God. Or his face, which was either all red, or white like
his hair. And the waves on his forehead, which was a little,
private beach beside the sea of the world.

It was then that I saw his neck. A deep wrinkle, almost
a crack, ran right across it. It was the first time that I saw

a deep, sun-scorched wadi, though I was still far away from Israel. Perhaps my father had also started out from just such a wadi. The rains hadn't come yet, and on that Yom Kippur the summer heat lay sweltering on the land where I had not yet been.

Only now do I see his face on the photograph that I keep in my closet. It is the face of a man who has started eating his favorite dish and is disappointed to find its flavor somewhat unsavory. The edges of his mouth, drooping at the corners, attest to this fact as do the wrinkles on his nose and the mute birds of sadness hovering in the corners of his eyes. I can collect a great deal of evidence from the face—not in order to pass judgment on him but to judge myself.

That Yom Kippur he stood in front of me, so very busy with his grown-up God. He was all white in his "shrouds." The entire world around him was black, like the charred stones left behind after a bonfire. The dancers were gone and the singers were gone, and only the blackened stones had remained. That's how my father, dressed in his white shroud, was left behind. It was the first time I remember my father dying.

When they got to the *aleinu* prayer, my father went down on his knees like all the others and touched the floor with his forehead. I thought he was drinking with his forehead, that maybe God flowed down there among the legs of the tables. Before he kneeled he spread out his velvet *tallit* bag so as not to get his knees dirty. He didn't worry about dirtying his forehead. Then he was resurrected. He got up without moving his feet, which he kept close together. He got up, and his face changed color a number of times and he was alive again and mine, and I climbed onto the seat to have a look at his neck and the wrinkle in it.

He was flesh and blood that was resurrected. Why are living people called flesh and blood? You only see flesh and blood when a man's been crushed, when his body is injured, or he's dead. When people are alive you see other combinations. You see not flesh and blood, but skin and eyes, a smile and dark hair, hands and a mouth.

I went up to the women's gallery to tell my mother about the resurrection. Up there they had apples filled with spices to keep the women from fainting. I envied the women. I have always wanted to faint but have never been able to—to be wiped off the board, to retreat from everything aimlessly and unresisting. The women were holding the spiced apples in their hands; I was also in their hands, and so was the entire globe. They held me up to the large clock to check the time with me. They looked at me in the light of the fires that were going to burn down the synagogue. From up there in the gallery I saw them stripping the white mantles off the scrolls of the law. They took hold of the shoulder straps and pulled the mantle off, leaving the scroll of the law naked and cold. Then my father came back to life, and in the evening he broke his fast after the ne'ilah service. The year was a huge wheel, a wall enclosing days and seasons. An odd game! My sins and my atonements were still folded up, and both of them looked the same. That evening, the moon circled the city like a gleaming white chicken used in the kapparot, the atonement ritual.

My father died many times more, and he still dies from time to time. Sometimes I am there, and sometimes he dies alone. Sometimes his death occurs quite near my table, or when I am working, writing pretty words on the blackboard or looking at the colorful countries on the map. But there are times when I am very far away when he dies, like the way it happened in the First World War. It's a good thing

THE TIMES MY FATHER DIED

sons don't see their fathers at war. And it's also a good thing that I wasn't in the same war, otherwise we might have killed one another; because he wore the uniform of Kaiser Wilhelm, while I wore the uniform of King George, God having put a gap of twenty-five years between us. I put his medals in the same box where I keep my own World War II decorations, as I had nowhere else to keep them. One of his medals has a lion on it and two swords crossed, as in a duel between two invisible swordsmen. Beasts of prey are prominent on most emblems: lions and eagles and bulls and hawks and all sorts of other ferocious creatures. In the synagogue they have a pair of lions holding up the tablets over the holy ark. Even our own laws, too, can only be protected and upheld by wild animals.

In Germany once, a long time after the war, my father put on a black frock coat and pinned on his decorations, then he donned a shiny top hat and went off to the dedication of a war monument. The names of all the dead were listed in alphabetical order. Where did the monument stand? In the public park near the playground, right next to the swings and sandboxes. I don't remember what the memorial looked like, but it must have had stone soldiers pointing stone rifles under stone flags, and stone mothers weeping stonily. There must also have been all sorts of wild beasts to immortalize the greatness of man and of his generals and emperors.

For four years my father died in the war. He dug a lot of trenches. They told him that sweat saves blood, and that the soldiers' blood saves the sweat of generals, and that the generals' sweat, in turn, saves the manufacturers and kaisers a lot of sweat and blood, and so on all down the line, a regular savings scheme. My father dug a lot of trenches, dug himself a whole lot of graves. He was wounded only once. All the other bullets and shrapnel missed. When he really died, many years later, all the bullets and pellets that had missed him got together and smashed his heart all at once; and that's how he never got out of the last trench, which others had dug for him. He went through a great many battles and was very often among those reported killed in action in the arithmetic of battle or those killed in the statistics of stormed positions. His blood glowed like those buttons you press to put on the electric light in apartment-house hallways, so that death should be able to see and light up his body with his blood. But death never pressed the buttons of his blood and my father didn't really die. God, in whom he believed, hovered over him like a white, saving parachute, high above the trajectory of the shells. He never involved his God in matters of war, but left Him among the laws of nature and the stars, above him, like a light foam which topped the dark, heavy beverage of his life.

Sometimes, when the war went hard, his body became like a tree that had shed its leaves. Only the branches of nerves remained, while his entire life dropped off like leaves. He sent back a great many letters from out there. At first the letters were infrequent, but during the four years of the war the letters accumulated into packs and bundles, and the packs hardened like stone. This is what happens to letters. At first they flutter in, fleet and white like a dove's wings; and later all the letters get hard like stone. The letters also wandered from storeroom to storeroom, from one chest of drawers to the other, into the closet and on top of the closet, and from there up to the attic and later right under the roof tiles. When my father really died, he leaped in one plunge much higher than his letters on the roof. When the real resurrection of the dead takes place, he will have to undo all those bundles and read out his letters. In his lifetime a man gives off a large quantity of sweat, blood, body waste, poetry, and letters.

Once he told us about some French prisoners of war at Verdun who asked him for water in their language (*de l'eau, de l'eau*), and he gave them all that was left in his water canteen. Since then I have never forgotten their calling out for water. Sometimes they come to me asking for a little water. Perhaps my father told them about me, but I hardly think so, since I wasn't born yet at the time. But in war—which jumbles people and earth together and throws everything into confusion, making people who are standing sit down, and those who are seated lie down, and turning the recumbent into pictures on the wall—in war everything is possible.

Once, just before Hitler came along, my father's former brothers-in-arms invited him to a regimental reunion. They sent him a nice letter on notepaper headed by the regimental emblem: a hunter's cap, antlers, and a couple of crossed rifles. Why did it have such an emblem? It was a hunting regiment with a glorious tradition behind it, a *corps d'élite*. Originally they used to hunt hares and stags; later they went hunting human beings in the war. Not just to hunt them, but actually to kill them. Nor was it to eat them, like one did hares, but simply to kill them and even to mangle their bodies, so that one could see flesh and blood, and not smiles and hair and arms and caresses and other fine combinations.

My father didn't accept the invitation and this, too, was death, because they liked him very much and used to call him David. During the war, they used to give him some of their rations on the Day of Atonement so that he might be able to fast. They would gather in the stars for his prayer and maintain moments of silence for his quiet devotions.

YEHUDA AMICHAI

In return he would keep their spirits up with his faith and with the funny stories he told.

After that he died frequently, a great many times.

He died when they came to arrest him for throwing into the garbage the Nazi pin I had found. The black uniforms came to our door. The black uniforms broke it down. And the boots tramped in. It was terrible for me to see that my father was no longer able to defend our house and withstand the enemy's onslaught. That was childhood's end. How could they just burst into our house like that against Father's wishes!

If I had been bigger then, I would have covered up my father as Shem did when he walked despondently.*

He died when they stationed bullies outside his shop to keep people from buying there because it was a Jewish shop.

He died when we left Germany to emigrate to Palestine, and all the years that had been died with him. When the train went past the Jewish Old Age Home, which my father had supported, all the old people stood waving their bedsheets from balconies and windows. They were not waving them in surrender but in farewell. There is no difference between surrender and goodbye, for in either case you wave white flags or handkerchiefs or even bedsheets.

He died a great many times, for he was made up of different materials. Sometimes he was like iron, sometimes like white bread, sometimes like antique wood, and all of these must die. There were times when I saw him cloaking his face with his hands so as not to let me see it stripped and bare. There were times when his thoughts overburdened his small body, and he sagged under their load. And

*See Gen. 10:23

there were times when he stood firm and strong like a chain of telephone poles, and his thoughts were wonderful, brilliant, and fleet like the stretched wires. Even the songbirds would then alight and perch on them.

When he really died, God didn't know whether he was really dead. Till then, he always used to rise from the dead, but this time he did not rise. A few weeks before he had had a heart attack. They call it a heart attack, but what attacks what? . . . does the heart attack the body, or the body the heart? Or does the world attack both?

When I came to see him one day, he was lying next to an iron oxygen bottle; his eyes were like the glass tumblers they crush underfoot at a wedding. When I went over to him, I heard the large oxygen bomb hissing. Once an angel stood next to the sickbed, but now there are bombs full of hissing oxygen. Sea divers and airplane pilots are also given oxygen tanks. Where was my father going? Was he going to dive, or go aloft maybe? At all events he was leaving us. He beckoned me over to him. I said, "Don't talk and tire yourself out," and he said, "There's the cat mewing on the neighbor's roof. Maybe it's shut in and wants to get out." I went over to the neighbor's to release the cat. And again all we heard was the hiss of the oxygen. There was a clock fitted onto the oxygen tank to measure the pressure. My father had as much time as the oxygen in the tank. My mother stood at the door. If only she had been able to, she would have stood at his bedside like the oxygen bomb giving him of her life force.

After that, my father slowly began to recover. Every day he regained a little of his color, as if all his colors had fled from his face and dispersed when his heart had been attacked and were now returning, like refugees after an air raid. The oxygen tank was put outside on the balcony.

The day he died they gave him a cardiogram. The doctor came and opened up a sort of radio and hooked it up to my father with all kinds of electric wires. When you love a person you don't need such a complicated gadget to examine his heart, but you do when somebody's ill. The needle traced zigzags on a roll of paper, like a seismograph in an earthquake. My father looked like a broadcasting station, completely covered with wires and antennas. That day he transmitted his last broadcast. I heard it.

The doctor said, "We're all right," as if anybody had doubted that he himself was all right too. He then dismantled the apparatus and showed us the zigzags, which he thought were all right.

In the evening I took my wife to see a movie. When the exaggerated faces on the screen had stopped laughing or crying, we went out to the street. My wife bought some flowers from a man who kept them in a bucket, just outside an artists' café. This place was frequented by sad-looking young poets who were forever gazing into the distance; men who sported a variety of battle pins; men who limped because of war injuries, and those who limped because it looked aristocratic; men who brandished moustaches; lovers of war in civilian clothes and peace lovers in uniform; and girls who liked keeping company with all of them. We bought red roses, possibly because we wanted to hasten the color to my father's cheeks.

We went back to sit down by my father's side. My wife put the flowers in a vase, where they breathed more freely. We drew up chairs around the bed and my father started telling us about a man who had arrived in the country after he had jumped off a train and had been hidden by good *goyim*. Tears welled up in my father's eyes as he spoke of the good people who had given shelter to a fugitive. His eyes filled with tears and an odd gurgling sound filled his mouth. His speech stopped all at once, like a film that snaps at the movies or like a radio program when another station suddenly cuts in. What other station could have cut in on my father's broadcast, causing both stations to go dead, his and the one that was making all the interference? His mouth opened wide, as if he still had a host of stories to tell about a lot of good people and his mouth couldn't get them all out at once. I rushed over to him, embraced him, and kissed his cold forehead. Perhaps I had just remembered that his forehead had once touched the ground on Yom Kippur— or did I wish to bring him back to life as Elisha had done? My mother came running in from the bathroom. My wife called the doctor. The doctor came and confirmed what was already a confirmed fact. A good neighbor came in and saw to the arrangements. A rabbi, an acquaintance of my father's, came in and supervised the rites; he had the furniture shifted around and windows opened and shut. He was used to people dying. He placed a lighted candle on the floor, like a lantern near a building that is going up or a road under repair. Then he opened a book and began whispering. The oxygen tank was no longer needed to whisper.

The next day they washed my father at home. They moved the furniture out of the room, poured out streams of water, and wrapped him in rolls of cloth. After he was buried, a whole lot of relatives and acquaintances came visiting. Aunt Shoshana came up from the country, glad to get away from her hundreds of chickens and meet friends she hadn't seen for a long time.

There were many occasions for mourning. We let pass the occasion for the loud, bitter wail of grief. Perhaps it was because he had died in the middle of telling a story, or because all the radio stations had suddenly closed down, or perhaps it was because the heart would have had to open up as wide as a trumpet mouth and it wasn't large enough for that. One could mourn with the shriek of the train that went up to Jerusalem through the oppressive, haunting mountains, or silently, like an unclosed window which silently suffers.

We have only a few facial expressions: sorrow, fear, a smile, and a few others, like the large mannequins in shop windows. Fate manipulates us, as a window dresser fixes his dummies into position, lifting an arm here and turning a head there, and that's the way they remain all through the season. It's the same with us.

I let my beard grow in mourning. At first it was bristly, but later it grew soft. Sometimes, when I lay down, I would hear shots or the rumble of tractors down in one of the valleys, or blasting from the stone quarries. My father was like those quarries; he gave me all his stone and depleted himself. Now that he was dead and I was built up, he remained gaping, void, and deserted, with the forest closing in around him. When I go down to the coastal plain sometimes, I see the stone quarries at the roadside, and they are deserted.

I ordered a tombstone. The evening before I went to order it I saw a girl standing near one of the tombstones, fixing her sandal strap. When she saw me coming she ran away between two tall buildings. I ordered a horizontal tombstone, with a stone pillow as a headpiece. The stonemason, like a tailor, asked me about measurements and seams and lines and materials.

The cemetery lies near the border. In times of crisis the dead are left to themselves, with only a few soldiers turning up from time to time. Next to my father lies a German doctor who doesn't have a tombstone but only a little tin marker. As you look toward the city you can see the Tnuva Dairy tower. Towers don't help us very much anymore, but the Tnuva tower is actually a refrigerator. There are also water towers which have to be high enough to fill all the houses with water. God, who is very high up, filled my father up to the brim.

I was filled with other things, and not always from high towers. Sometimes the pressure was weak and I was only half filled with dreams and ideas. I was in the cemetery a few days ago. Each grave bears a name and a verse. No one knows where Moses was buried, but we know where he lived and we still know all about his life. Nowadays everything is the other way around. We know only where the burial places are. Where we live is unfixed and unknown. We roam about, we change, we shift. Only the burial place is known.

I, for my part, go my way, developing some of my father's qualities and some of his facial features and traits. I develop some, and discard others.

But, as I have said at the beginning, my father still keeps dying. He comes to me in my dreams and I am afraid for him and say: Take your coat, walk more slowly, don't talk, you mustn't get excited, take a rest from this awful war. I myself can't rest. I must keep going, but not to pray. I place my phylacteries, not on my arm and forehead, but in the drawer which I never open anymore.

Once I was walking along the ancient Appian Way in Rome. I was carrying my father on my shoulders. Suddenly his head sagged and I was afraid he was going to die. I laid him down at the side of the road and put a stone under his head, and went to call a taxi. Once they used to call on

God to help; now you call a taxi. I couldn't find one, and I got farther away from my father. Every few steps I would turn around to look at him, then run on toward the stream of traffic. I saw him lying by the roadside; only his head was turned in my direction, following me. I saw him through the ancient arch of San Sebastian. Passersby stopped, bent over him, and then went on. I finally got a taxi, but it was too narrow and looked like a snake. I got another one, and the driver said: "We know him; he's only pretending to be dead." I turned around and saw that my father was still lying by the side of the road, his white face turned to me. But I didn't know if he was still alive. I turned around again and saw him, a very distant object, through the ancient arches of San Sebastian's gate.

Translated by Yosef Schachter

Acknowledgments

Hebrew Short Stories: An Anthology in Two Volumes, selected by S.Y. Penueli and A. Ukhmani. Volume Two; Tel Aviv: Institute for the Translation of Hebrew Literature and Megiddo Publishing Co., 1965. For "The Times My Father Died." *Modern Hebrew Stories* (A Bantam Dual-Language Book), edited by Ezra Spicehandler. New York: Bantam Books, 1971. For "The Times My Father Died." *Omer II. An Anthology of Contemporary Hebrew Literature,* selected and edited by David Hardan.￯ (Cultural Division, Department for Education and Culture in the Diaspora, and Institute for the Translation of Hebrew Literature, edited by Robert Alter.) New York: Behrman House, 1975. For "The Times My Father Died." *Israeli Stories. A Selection of the Best Contemporary Hebrew Writing,* edited by Joel Blocker. New York: Herzl Press, 1962; New York: Schocken Books, 1965. For "Battle for the Hill." *Penguin Modern Stories 7,* edited by Judith Burnley. Harmondsworth: Penguin Books, 1971. For "Battle for the Hill." *Contemporary Israeli Literature,* edited by Elliott Anderson. Philadelphia: The Jewish Publication Society of America, 1977. For "The Orgy."

Several of these stories originally appeared in: *Commentary, Midstream, Modern Hebrew Literature* (Tel Aviv), and *TriQuarterly.*